Curse of the Maestro and Other Stories

G T Walker

Copyright 2024 by MSI Press LLC

All rights reserved. No part of this book may be reproduced or utilized in any form or by any means, electronic or mechanical, including photocopying and recording, or by any information storage and retrieval system without permission in writing from the publisher.

For information, contact
MSI Press, LLC
1760-F Airline Hwy #203
Hollister, CA 95023

Copyeditor: Betty Lou Leaver
Cover design & layout: Opeyemi Ikuborije
ISBN: 978-1-957354-44-6
LCCN: 2024918126

CONTENTS

Acknowledgements. 1

Curse of the Maestro. 3

Older than Beethoven: The Stonehaven Symphony Wiki. 21

Mistress to the Music 29

Backstage Peeps 41

Star-cross'd. 55

The Rocky Mountain Cochlea 77

Curious George and His Little Brown Bugle. 93

Sticky Notes 97

The Gingerbread Man 111

Musicians Do Care 133

Haute Plains Drifter 147

The Visitors 161

ACKNOWLEDGEMENTS

The list of those who supported the creation of these stories is somewhat shorter than the list of all those who contributed to making me the kind of person who would write such things. Is this a good time to mention any resemblance to actual persons, living or dead, or actual events is purely coincidental? Anyway, I'd also like to thank Karin Park, Hoosier Lit, Points In Case, and the staff of MSI Press including Dr. Betty Lou Leaver and Opeyemi Ikuborije, without whom this book would have never been… what it is.

CURSE OF THE MAESTRO

> *Is it true great music never dies? Do the dead keep musical secrets? Have you ever seen a dead person?*
>
> *Tutamen's Curse of the Maestro™ touring museum exhibit answers these questions and more. Museum patrons will witness the complicated lives and unsurprising deaths of 49 young musicians. Go on a journey of exploration! Experience the magnificent artifacts of Maestro Michel Butrie, his star-crossed Stonehaven Symphony orchestra, and the early 21st Century archaeologist who discovered them all—Dame Haylie Cartwright!*

Museum exhibitions devoted to cultural history and music have dwindled in popularity for many years, so often due to their pretentious irrelevance. But Curse of the Maestro presents this fascinating subject in an entirely new way. This immersive exhibit allows visitors to re-live the events of the famous 2018 Stonehaven Symphony Tour Bus excavation. Colorado artisans and taxidermists have lovingly recreated Michel Butrie's earthly possessions as well as the remains of orchestra musicians and livestock that followed him into the afterlife. A variety of educational materials are on display. See the mock conductor's podium, complete with rehearsal sticky notes. Children are given brightly colored activity handouts, with quizzes and games that simulate the gigging musician's daily life from cradle to grave. You'll be guided by a free audio tour based on the Dame Cartwright diaries, read educational wall panels, and watch historical re-enactments featuring local school children. Here at the Colorado Museum of Nature and Science, guided tours are also provided twice weekly by enthusiastic Mountain Vista Women's Correctional Facility residents.

Interactive kiosks feature an actual 21st Century musician's journal, cell phone transcripts, drug prescriptions, all manner of rusty musical instruments, a Pokémon list, newspaper clippings and reviews, a tattoo transcription, more sticky notes, program notes, a summons, letters, laptop drives, and an ankle monitor. Audio guide headphone tours are narrated by the official exhibit mascot, Trumpet Monkey. After blowing chocolates out of a toy horn, he always leads children straight to the Haylie Cartwright Diary Room

The Haylie Cartwright Diary Room

Haylie Cartwright's biography is unique among archaeologists. She was a fearless and feisty inspiration for women of all ages. Haylie was 23 years old in 2018, fresh out of archaeology school. A tall, red-headed vegan and entry-level banjoist, Haylie left the UK to immerse herself in the burgeoning Rocky Mountain Bluegrass scene. At the time, the Denver Musicians Union was experiencing a financial downturn. Many musicians, living in poverty, were unable to pay union dues. In desperation and in hopes of recovering past due payments from recently deceased members, the Denver Musicians Union had just posted a new job description: Musical Paleontologist. Young Haylie jumped at the opportunity for employment.

Haylie's archeological team consisted of personal secretary/estranged girlfriend Riia Bethard, Denver Musicians Union treasurer and newly appointed Colorado Wind Quintet Flautist Louden Carnard, as well as a fluid number of Sigma Alpha Iota music sorority girls. Intern Li'l Willy Williams appeared to be responsible for most of the actual digging. Most of the team's curated objects were excavated in Glenwood Springs' Valley of the Orchestras, two alpine canyons on the west bank of the Colorado River, 156 miles west of Denver. Covering half a square mile, the valley is the site of some 62 orchestra tour bus fatalities.

> *Haylie recorded her activities in her journal, and this diary is exhibited among her own effects, including reading glasses, a pink banjo plectrum, and a well-used roach clip. The original diary and its annotations have been painstakingly edited by her faithful secretary, Riia. They are all visible in a glass display case, opened on the entry for 1 August 2018, the very day of Haylie's big discovery. The transcript is presented here with only minor redactions for a family audience.*

<u>Bus discovery.</u>
<u>Wednesday, July 28.</u>

Riia is not in the mood for snuggles.

Can't sleep/get comfortable on my side of the tent. My left leg is restless. It's also cold. Dozed for a bit. Rummaging around for some chewing gum. Still somewhat gaseous after a fortnight of Coors and artisanal wildflower jerky.

My tummy growled like a Rottweiler until about 5:00 am when Riia reared up and cast me out into the night.

Outside the tent extricating myself from the shattered remains of my banjo, I sprang to my feet. Brilliant. This had all been her idea. The trip had been a chance to take a break from her own research at the Paleopathology Association, a romantic little archaeological getaway, digging up dead guys, just the two of us snuggle bunnies. Fair enough, it was I who thought Hegelbach should send along Louden Carnard to see where the Musicians Union money was going, but the Sigma Alpha Iota girls were already here when we arrived. Engaged in some manner of elaborate hazing ceremony. Blindfolds/marijuana/salmon. And we also needed Li'l Willy. She knew that. What else were we supposed to do? Because R. hates shovels. The hole wasn't going to dig itself.

I brushed myself off. I started walking, I did not know where. In search of warmth. Or a quiet place on which to urinate. It was quite early; the night sky had already begun to blush. The full moon had disappeared down the other side of the canyon.

The front flap of Louden Carnard's vacant pup tent was fluttering in the evening's breeze. A short distance downstream, the contents of the Sigma Alpha Iota tent were silhouetted from within. Bodily noises and giggles and scantily clad male/female body parts. And there was a pepperoni scent. Somebody had smuggled animal products into our encampment. R. was a staunch animal rights advocate, and she was going to be furious. God help the blighters if R. finds any lunch meats on that Louden Carnard. Wanker! My intestines knotted at the thought. I nursed my flickering lamp onward. Clambered the barren ridge opposite our encampment. There, downslope from the interstate lights, there was a shadowy outline of shrubbery. With all due urgency, I positioned myself behind the most substantial cactus. I hastily lowered my bottoms and prepared to release the kraken.

At that moment, I became aware of a low, rasping snarl.

It was a guttural sound, as if Mother Earth Herself was parting between my feet in inarticulate protest. I uneasily adjusted the stream. Then, I felt the delicate puff of breath just off my right cheek. The lamp dropped from my fingers. Bollocks! So, there in the darkness, I ever-so-carefully stepped back into the pajamas pooled at my feet. As I inched them back up into due modesty, I saw the creature behind my right foot.

The hideous writhing beast was two metres long and half again in breadth. It was whistling like a flatulent anaconda. It was as strong an argument for veganism as I have ever seen. But it was Li'l Willy in a mummy bag.

A swift kick silenced the snoring. The intern's nappy head popped out the zipper.

"Your biotch, Riia," he cried, eyes rolling back in his head, "she of the Devil!"

Curled up in his sleeping bag between the cactus and an old truck tire, Li'l Willy was a pathetic sight. While I remain a staunch supporter of animal rights, Riia literally prefers livestock to men, and this is why. Come to find out the previous evening she had discovered Li'l Willy's clandestine expedition to a local fast-food establishment. She had proceeded to beat the carnivorous skank with his own Happy Meal. And now he was banished to the far side of the valley. Was it an overreaction on R.'s part? Perhaps. R. had grown prickly in the wake of fledgling experiments with anhydrous ammonia first obtained at annual Paleopathology Association meetings in Cancun.

I looked down at him lying there in the underbrush, lips turning blue, a tinny pulsation of Tupac from his earbuds. But at that moment, I noticed the diminutive intern's eyes widen. He suddenly began to thrash about, pointing behind me and down the slope. I turned around and looked back at the other cacti, now illuminated with a beam from the fallen flashlight. There, ten metres above the river bed was a pair of long serrated ruts in the dirt, the unmistakable skid marks of a wayward tour bus.

Willy and I scrambled down the incline for a closer look. Quite a short time sufficed to reveal the beginning of a steep excavation cut into the bedrock about four metres south of the remnants of a guardrail and a similar depth below the current level of the valley.

We presently alerted the Sigma Alpha Iota girls and commenced working. It took the whole of this day to free this excavation before the lower margins of the skid marks could be demarcated. Indeed, it was getting late, night had fast set in, and the full moon had risen high in the eastern heavens. In the near distance, a pack of common mountain coyotes could be heard howling into the wind. In high spirits, we lit our pipes and resumed the previous evening's debauchery.

> *Founded circa 1093 A.D., most likely in Ankhetaten (present-day Eastern Slope, Colorado), the Stonehaven Symphony originally evolved from an expedition of itinerant Viking explorers who had learned to play musical instruments. They were first called "Svinhqfdi kamp" by the American Indian people who did not like them very much. Historians say these early musicians would take vows, promise to forget everything they had ever learned, and play along with whoever had the white stick. By 2008 A.D., that man was Michel Butrie. The young maestro was probably the thirteenth or fourteenth director of the orchestra; his reign appears to have lasted all of four years. He was known to be a well-meaning but rather dull ruler, so it may have seemed longer than that. Then, some time that fall, while enroute to the town of Beaver Creek, the Stonehaven Symphony tour bus driver drove off a cliff. It was a tragic day in music history. Butrie and his orchestra were not actually reported missing for several months. That all changed when in early December of 2013, several elderly subscription ticket holders noticed nobody was on the stage*

> *It remained for the secrets of the maestro's obscurity to finally be paraded for all to see that fateful July night when Riia Bethard, Dame Haylie Cartwright's personal secretary/estranged girlfriend, exposed the front bumper of Butrie's long-lost tour bus.*

Thursday, July 29.

That night, weed was smoked, backs were rubbed, and mistakes were made.

Not sure how I ended up in the hammock beside Louden Carnard's pup tent. I do remember waking to an eerie sensation: a coyote pup nibbling on my lower abdomen. Regaining consciousness, I dislodged the beast, slid back into my swimwear, and surveyed the excavation site. It was mid-morning. My carefully triangulated pin flags were strewn across the clearing. A gaggle of Sigma Alpha Iota girls were playing hacky sack with the artifact bags. Grabbing my trusty pickaxe, I approached the southern quadrant of the excavation.

Archaeological material tends to accumulate in protrusions. Each protrusion, which may have taken a short or long time to accumulate, leaves a context. This layer cake of protrusions is often referred to as an archaeological sequence or record. It is by analysis of this sequence or record that excavation can lead to interpretation, which in turn may lead to discussion and understanding.

Riia had been assigned a simple yet time-consuming task: digging a volleyball pit. There had been no complex dictation for us to get in a fight about, no intellectual challenge; this was simply something that would keep her out of the Sigma Alpha Iota tent. But there she was, now digging Louden Carnard. L.C. was reclining by the creek, flute in one hand, R. in the other, his white skeletal rib cage puffed out in the morning's sun, engaged in an insouciant demonstration of Baroque tonguing.

My intestinal knot returned with a vengeance. Bloody hell. R. hated men. At least live ones. Naturally, as a paleopathologist, R. always had a thing for classical musicians, but I thought they had to be dead first. She had told me she loved me. She told me she loved running her fingers through my hair after a vigorous shag. She told me we would always be together. Fair enough, she also liked to say she loved sinking her gloves into freshly-opened mummies.

I demanded to know why the excavation had not been completed. R. replied that she had started to dig but had then run up against a large jutting protrusion. "A jutting protrusion, as in archaeological material," I asked, my excitement beginning to mount. "Where?" I demanded. She then glanced longingly at L.C. before they both giggled and she adjusted her thong.

Amidst L.C.'s simpering interpretation of full responsibility, I became aware of the pickaxe in my hand.

(Redacted)

After the police officers left, my archeological team cleared down to the level of the vehicle's front bumper, sufficient to expose a large part of the upper portion of a crumpled grill, mud flaps, and windshield. We had worked unceasingly through the afternoon, without pause for food or drink or recreational substances or urgent urination. Here before us was sufficient evidence to show that it really was another tour bus crash site, and, to all outward appearances, intact save a glass segment apparently fractured by an impact from within. By the time we meticulously exposed portions of the front windshield, though, I was satisfied that I was on the verge of perhaps a magnificent find, probably one of the missing buses that I had been seeking for many weeks. Had I known that by digging a few inches deeper I would have exposed the moldering skull of its sleepy bus driver, I probably would have voided my nether bits. As it was, it was getting late. The night had fast set in, and the full moon had risen high in the eastern heavens. I refilled the excavation for protection, and with the Sigma Alpha Iota contingent selected for the occasion—they like myself delighted beyond expectation—I returned back to my tent and cabled to the Musicians Union the following message:

"At last, have made wonderful discovery in the Valley of a magnificent bus with mud flaps intact recovered same for your arrival congratulations."

> *So where did "The Curse" come from?*
>
> *According to the Epic Mountain Dispensary website, "When the Stonehaven Symphony Tour Bus Crash Site was discovered and excavation began in 2018, it was a major archaeological event. In order to keep the public and press at bay and yet allow them a sensational aspect for future funding opportunities, the head of the excavation team, Haylie Cartwright, promoted the story that a curse had been placed upon anyone who violated the resting place of the maestro. Dame Cartwright did not invent the idea of an ancient, cursed tomb, but she did exploit it to keep intruders away from her history-making discovery."*
>
> *Of course, a number of mysterious deaths followed, but they can all be explained with explanations.*

Friday, July 30.

As word of the discovery spread, friends old and new began to arrive. A delegation from the Epic Mountain Dispensary made an appearance. Olivia and her Red Rocks Community College roommates showed up. They came in station wagons and motorhomes, arriving on horseback and by canoe. Our fledging camp has tripled in size. The Carbondale Bluegrass Boys came and set up a make-shift stage just below the highway. Now every morning we awake to the melody of what sounds like the violent restringing of a dozen banjos.

Not coincidentally, Riia has become increasingly unstable. Given to volatile mood shifts and nonsequital sighs. Still hasn't forgiven me for powdering Louden Carnard's flute. Disappears into our tent, which has since converted into a primitive meth lab, for hours at a time and cranks up "Die Zauberflöte" when approached. Haven't seen L.C. since he disappeared into the Sigma Alpha Iota tent for an impromptu lip exercise workshop last night. He is a wanker. Must protect R. from L.C. and herself.

My old wing gal Zion from Liverpool rolled in on her Harley. She grabbed my pickaxe and immediately began to gut away, reaching as far as the femur in the driver's seat. Li'l Willy, still in the throes of methamphetamine withdrawal, has become unduly amused with the bone. He is running and tossing it up and down in the meadow. "Fly, fly, the butterfly!," he shouts.

We found masses of broken potsherds, dark flint and chert stones in the lower rubbish that filled the stairwell entrance. L.C. has finally emerged from the Sigma Alpha Iota tent looking none the worse for the wear. Wanker. But emboldened now that the pickaxe is now safely out of my reach, he grabbed a trowel and got to work. As we cleared the glove compartment, we found mixed with the rubble broken potsherds, jar seals, and numerous fragments of small objects; small lambskin sheaths lying on the floorboard together with alabaster jars, whole and broken, and coloured pottery vases; all pertaining to some disturbed burial. These were disturbing elements as they pointed toward plundering.

We sat down together with L.C. by the creek and ate warm tofu and acorn bread with a thermos of vegan kimchi. No one said a word. As was his custom, L.C. removed his shirt. More of a buffalo wing gal, Z.'s eyes began to water as she forced down a chewy curd then reached for the brew with shaking hands. I was preoccupied. My mind spinning with the implications of the treasures we had unearthed. What did it all mean, I finally asked. L.C. had fallen asleep. Z. said that she did not know, then excused herself to vomit.

> *The first of the "mysterious" deaths was that of William "Li'l Willy" Williams (1993-2018). The fun-loving intern had been bitten by a mosquito in the meadow. He later slashed the bite accidentally while shaving his head. It became infected, and blood poisoning resulted. It was a tragic coincidence. For those who knew him, Li'l Willy will be remembered as a strong man, a quietly courageous man, who simply had the misfortune of always being the company of women who were stronger and more courageous. For those who did not know him, he probably won't be remembered at all. Evidently that included quite a few people because it took several days for him to die; then several more passed before the Cartwright team was aware of his absence, which then prompted Dame Cartwright's now famous words, "Well what are we waiting for, this hole isn't going to dig itself!"*

Word of the discovery continues to spread, and our little Tour Bus Crash Site community has grown. Hegelbach, the Chief Inspector of the local Musicians Union Antiquities Dept., drove up from Denver with Bruford and the Symphonic Department officers. The Symphonic Department had absolutely filled his old pickup with hunting paraphernalia. H. was on hand to witness the freeing of the rubbish from the engine cavity.

He stuck his thickly bearded head inside the bus and sniffed around. 'You sure they're dead?'

Louden Carnard replied in the affirmative.

"Well, their membership is past due. They got fines to pay," he insisted, whereupon L.C. reminded him they'd be dead for quite some time. "They got stuff in there. Fiddles, gold teeth, anything we can pawn," he said. "Truck needs brakes."

I replied that it would not be prudent to attempt entry, given the fragile condition of the artifacts.

He grabbed me by the scruff of the neck, "Haylie, you send your girls down in there and you git it. I don't care if you have to rip it from their cold dead fingers."

And with that he and the Symphony Department, save Brudford, vanished up into the woods with their firearms, damp squibs to a man. Save Bruford, whom one could always count on for a couple pounds of prime-grade hashish.

Which we did.

Thus girded, I did reconcile with a downcast L.C. He had tired of Alpha Sigma Iota girls and was heard to say that he had always appreciated my own intellectual precosity and tireless inquisition. The sound of semi-automatic weapons and the screeching of wildlife echoed in the background as the sun set below the mountains. I, too, was forced to acknowledge that while I would dread my own estranged girlfriend's reaction, L. did have a certain hollow-cheeked appeal. I did apologize for pickaxing his flute and resolved to support his remaining oral ambitions in any way I could. A compelling expression inched across his cadaverous smile, and I submitted that while I was differently orientated and a vegetarian, there might be a way to set aside my various convictions long enough to get some meat on his bones. We thereupon lost the plot and spent the night in the meadow.

<u>Saturday, July 31.</u>
<u>(Unintelligible)</u>

<u>Sunday, August 1.</u>

I awoke with a start: it was three o'clock in the afternoon. I found myself in the meadow, near the nine-angled satanic circle that had been burnt into the grass around the perimeter of the site. Recoiling from the half-eaten coyote kabob in my hand, I sprang to my feet and surveyed the carnage of men, women, and livestock sleeping on the ground around me in various stages of denudement. Louden Canard was nowhere to be found. But there, nursing the embers of what appeared to be a primitive barbecue pit at the center of my excavation, on the front bumper of my bus, sat Hegelbach.

He laughed mightily before walking over and snatching the small carcass from my hands. He relished a tyrannical bite.

"The Symphony Department gunned this one down last night. Wasn't easy to get a clear shot what with all those li'l pups around her. Last I heard, the boys said they was gonna go blow up a rabbit. Wonder where they're at now."

Tears ran down my face. I happened to glance over toward that tent I'd shared with Riia. The open canvas flap fluttered to reveal a now vacant interior. At that moment, the image of a meth-addled vegan swinging down through the trees occurred to my mind.

"They're already dead." I replied.

Bruford and I returned to the wreck's stairwell and driver's quarters. Both in plan and style, they resembled almost to measurement the tour bus containing whatever remained of the Philadelphia Youth Orchestra discovered by in the very near vicinity last season. Feverishly, we cleared away the remaining last scraps of rubbish on the floor of the passage before the driver's seat until only a dripping wall of sediment and plastered orchestral sheet music stood between us and the sealed passenger area. After making preliminary notes, we made a tiny breach in the top left-hand corner to see what was beyond. Darkness and the iron testing rod told us that there was empty space. Perhaps a wet bar area, as per touring union orchestra accommodations? Or maybe a group toilet? Candles were procured—the all-important tell-tale for foul gases when opening an ancient subterranean excavation—and I widened the breach and by means of the candle looked in, while Bruford, Zion, the

Sigma Alpha Iota girls, the Carbondale Bluegrass Boys and Hegelbach waited in anxious expectation.

> *Robert Buttrell Hegelbach (1963-2020), Chief Inspector, American Musicians Union Antiquities, passed away years later after he supposedly threw himself off his seventh-floor apartment. Once again, this "mysterious death" was an unhappy coincidence. As was the unfortunate fact that, like the barbequed cuisine he loved so well, he was shish kabobbed on the wrought iron railing below. Inspector Hegelbach will be forever remembered as a straight-shooter with a heart of gold who knew how to finish in the black. Foul play is not suspected. A curse is not a real thing. After all, he had shown signs of mental instability following the Cartwright Expedition.*
>
> *And, of course, his treasurer's tragic discovery.*

It was sometime before one could see the hot air escaping caused the candle to flicker, but as soon as one's eyes became accustomed to the glimmer of light the interior of the chamber gradually loomed before one with its strange and wonderful medley of extraordinary and beautiful objects heaped upon one another.

There was naturally short suspense for those present who could not see, when Hegelbach said to me, "Can you see anything of value."

I replied to him, "Yes, it is wonderful."

I then with precaution made the hole sufficiently large for us both to see. With the light of an electric torch as well as an additional candle, we looked in. Our sensations and astonishment are difficult to describe as the better light revealed to us the marvelous collection of treasures: hangers of sumptuous concert dresses and guacamole-stained formal wear; two strange gleaming instruments of brass, evidently impaling the ceiling overhead; potato-coated upholstery in strange forms; exquisitely stickered violin cases; sheet music; sticky notes; some beautifully executed device of lotus and papyrus; an inflatable doll; drums and rattles; and strange wire stands—black shrines with a gilded monster snake appearing from within; quite ordinary looking white chests; finely carved chairs; a gold-inlaid throne; scattered decks of playing cards and gilded electronic gaming devices; a heap of large curious white oviform boxes; beneath our very eyes, on the threshold, a lovely lotiform wishing-cup in translucent alabaster; stools of all shapes and design, of both common and rare materials; a confusion of overturned parts of chariots glinting with gold and on either side of one more still-sealed doorway, the goat mummies. The first impression suggested the property-room of a theatre from a vanished civilization.

We questioned one another as to the meaning of it all. There was no sign of inhabitants or their earthly remains. It appeared as if an entire bus load of musicians had vanished as into the sulfurous air. It was a mystery. Perhaps the only possible clue to their demise was the tell-tale coyote droppings and a breeze wafting up from the forward lavatory where mangled bodies had been dragged out by the wildlife years before.

Our sensations were bewildering and full of strange emotion. What did it all mean? Was this a tomb or merely a cache? Where was that smell coming from? And why was the lifeless face of Louden Carnard peering from amongst the goat mummies?

Indeed, the expression in his sightless eyes was somewhat familiar from the previous night's romp. Lips pursed as if reaching for my ear lobe, or a high flute note. He looked as if he was about to say something, or remember. Fair enough, it did look somewhat more like he had been smothered while gasping for air; he was wearing the remains of a pepperoni pizza box around his neck and the expression of a man who had been trying to chew his way out.

The sensations the team was experiencing were bewildering and full of strange emotion. I knew mine were. It's always sobering to find the body of an ex-lover. Certainly, this wasn't the first time this kind of thing had happened since Riia became my soul partner, but it always kind of took my breath away. A sealed doorway between the two gilded goat mummies proved there was more beyond, and with the numerous cartouches bearing the name of Michel Butrie on most of the objects before us, there was little doubt that there behind was the private sleeping quarters of that maestro, and with it, the magnificent interment of discovery, fame, and recognition that awaits us all. For inside every stained tuxedo, there is a story waiting to be told.

OLDER THAN BEETHOVEN: THE STONEHAVEN SYMPHONY WIKI

> *Screenshot c. 2013*
>
> *In the early 21st century, "Wiki" was a funny, slang word for pages on the Wikipedia website. Lovingly assembled by contributors over many years, the Stonehaven Symphony's entry was a happy compilation of the organization's proudest achievements. Beginning with a description of the orchestra's prehistoric origins, highlights include accounts of the ensemble's 19th century exploits, and a succession of illustrious music directors culminating in the arrival of the Maestro himself, Michel Butrie, DMA.*

Slope, Colorado's Stonehaven Symphony is a fully professional orchestra that has long been a leader in the musical life of the area's metro region. Founded in 1958, the Stonehaven Symphony may be heard in performance on the University of Colorado campus and tours spanning five counties, over 13 local cities and ski towns, and dozens of area schools and auditoriums. In October 2012, the Symphony, led by Music Director Michel Butrie, DMA, made its Mountainview Women's Correctional Facility debut. As early as February 2003, the musicians under the baton of then-Maestro Enrico Splashowski gave a historic performance at the Panesville Reptile House, the first visit there by an American orchestra. Closely watched by herpetologists around the world, this achievement ultimately garnered the orchestra the coveted 2004 In Cold Blood Award for Cultural Diplomacy. Indeed, the ensemble's at times implausible ascent may be traced back to humble beginnings almost 1000 years ago.

"Humble Beginnings:" 1093 A.D.

While the Stonehaven Symphony was founded in 1958, anthropologists have traced its roots back to a small expedition of Viking adventurers, possibly refugees from Erik the Red's Newfoundland trek. Archeological evidence suggests the early hominids had arrived at the steppes of what is now Eastern Slope during the spring of 1093. Contemporary excavations have produced remarkably well-preserved skeletal remains, including the endocranial cast of a brain and a tiny skull. The specimen reveals an opposable thumb and the partially chewed portion of foramen magnum, evidence of bipedal locomotion. All these traits confirm the "Slope Man" was an evolutionary ancestor, perhaps a transitional link between musicians and modern humans. In fact, this early Cro-Magnon was immortalized by the petroglyphs left behind perhaps moments before meeting his fate at the furry hands of the world's earliest music critics.

The mountain thaw was well underway, flowers were blooming and small rodents dashed across the hillside as the expedition came over the rise. At that moment, the Vikings, still inebriated with a heavy store of fermented berries acquired near Cape Bauld, set eyes upon the unspoiled wasteland of present-day Slope. Imagine the sight surrounding indigenous Native American peoples beheld as the grief-stricken adventurers hurled vials of berry beverages at each other and the wildlife, cries of *"Svinhqfdi kamp!"* (either "Swine head carrion!" or "Symphony club!") filling the air.

This spectacle would eventually evolve into regularly programmed concerts/rodent sacrifices that grew in popularity. Archaeological evidence of the Slope Man's ancient program notes abounds ("*Fingr tunga góðr!*", also Old Norse, English: "finger licking good," petroglyph, 1093 AD). Of course, these early hominids were just pounding on rocks, but they already felt quite cultured and superior to the surrounding indigenous peoples who eventually lost patience and slaughtered them, also in 1093.

"Bach, Beethoven, and Badminton:" 1833 A.D.

Through the centuries, this irrepressible Aryan *joie de vivre* never waned. After the founding of Slope municipality in 1831, a Civic Symphony Orchestra was officially inaugurated, one phase of a new recreational program in a plan adopted by the city council: "Bach, Beethoven, and Badminton" (March 4, 1833, Eastern Slope Pioneer Gazette headline).

On the evening of March 4, 1833, Slope Auditorium was filled to capacity. One eyewitness reported, "Never has the hall been so full or so resplendent; the stairways and the corridors were crowded with spectators eager to see and to hear."

The program began with Johann Sebastian Bach's *Sinfonia in F major*. During his lifetime, Johann Sebastian Bach's music was widely considered "artificial and laborious." By March 4, 1833, he'd been dead 80 years.

Beethoven's "Egmont Overture" fared somewhat better though the string section's opening phrase had seemed simultaneously precipitous and tentative. It was the dappled tittering that greeted the oboe solo which foreshadowed the evening's demise.

An elderly couple, possibly recalling the previous week's impromptu "Badminton Massacre," rose from their front row seats. At that point, a "terrific uproar" was heard from above. Local music writers had stopped up the restroom urinals, which began to overflow from the balcony stage right. Veteran ticket scalper Carl Van Vechten reported that one individual was carried away with excitement and "began to beat rhythmically on top of my head," though Van Vechten failed to notice this at first, his own emotion being so great. Bassoonist Theodore Peach would later testify that the trouble escalated when members of the audience began to physically attack one another. Their mutual anger soon coalesced upon the orchestra itself: "Everything available was tossed in our direction, but we continued to play until we finally took on water."

On a positive note, the city's badminton rankings continued to flourish, thanks to the magnificent natural terrain and a tradition of offering visiting teams the lower half of a playing court that resembled a luge run. The orchestra, however, would soon disband. An insurmountable loss of personnel had occurred, due first to the Blizzard of '34, then boredom, then the **Nordic Venereal Plague**, also of '34.

The "Renaissance" Years: 1956-58

Bassoonist Isidore Polansky (nee Peach), husband Buddy, and other volunteer musicians revived the orchestra during the summer of 1956, not long before the arrival of Wilhelm Stonehaven Jr., from New York City. Previously something of a man-about-town and provocateur, Stonehaven's grandfather had just died, bequeathing to him sole ownership of the same local butcher shop which employed Mr. Buddy Polansky. At first, small town life appeared to have little to offer such a cosmopolitan gentleman. Upon making Mr. Polansky's acquaintance and nonetheless, Wilhelm learned the local philharmonic boasted a favorable male-to-female ratio. Gramps' old viola presently resurfaced, and the budding virtuoso began to attend rehearsals. It was his initial introduction to perhaps more grizzled members of the Symphony Ladies Guild, however, that inspired the young man to coin the official orchestra motto, "Older than Beethoven."

In the absence of audition requirements, little is known of Stonehaven's actual facility. He is said to have drawn his bow with a wax-like inaudibility, as if attentive to those around him. Perhaps it was this extraordinary musical sensitivity which enabled the future maestro to accompany the fairer sex of the ensemble. In fact, it was only a matter of months before the dashing young man was voted Artistic Director, not long after that demonstrating a preference for married bassoonists in the presumed privacy of the Slope Auditorium green room. His audibly tumescent appreciation was not lost upon those volunteers arriving to set chairs for that evening's rehearsal. Tragically, his tenure was to last only until the following weekend's gala celebration, when Wilhelm Stonehaven Jr. was discovered in two men's room stalls.

The "Golden Era:" 1958-2008

The organization's Golden Era was largely forged by a succession of three towering figures:

Timothy Moffat Childs IV, "The Child King" (1958-1997). An artist small in stature but mighty in musical vision. From the spring of his podium debut, blessed with only a freshly stamped baccalaureate, his boyish charm outweighed any possible Napoleonic complexes, and audiences doubled. The newly re-named Stonehaven Symphony attained professional union standing. Patrons celebrated the unforgettable experience of watching a conductor mature and grow before their eyes like a musical sea monkey. But at the apex of success, his fairytale marriage to a music school sweetheart ended. The alimony settlement alone fairly crushed the man. Indeed, few will forget that season's impassioned account of Franz Joseph Haydn's Symphony No. 83, "The Hen." But Childs had raised the ensemble's artistry to unimagined heights. Local concertgoers will forever remember his witty repartee, the earnestness of his gesticulation, and the question of whether or not he would ever grow tall enough to see over the podium. Then came that sunny spring day when he arrived at rehearsal sporting generously heeled elevator loafers. As he strode onto the podium platform, the maestro was able to see the musicians over his score lamp for the first time. Overcome by the sight of his ex-wife subbing in the second violin section, he cast down his baton, stormed out of the rehearsal, never to be heard from again. During the restructuring phase that followed, the organization swung from guest conductor to guest conductor, Orchestra Board members went into hiding, and subscriptions plummeted. What the organization needed more than anything else was a steady hand at the proverbial tiller, a man's man who could plow the sinking soil of musicality to new depths.

Zoltan "Iron Lip" Vegh (1997-2007). As it turned out, few men had a hand steadier than that of the stoic Hungarian, Maestro Zoltan Vegh. Anecdotal evidence suggests he once enjoyed an illustrious career as principal horn for one of the Big Five orchestras. Legend had it that he never cracked a single note in his fifty-year tenure. Eventually, he resigned his position and retired to the Rocky Mountain region in the early '90s following the automobile accident which severed his upper lip. Many of the Symphony's brass section had grown up listening to his recordings. They sought him out and lobbied for his appointment, enthralled by his reputation as an uncompromising, meticulous artist with nerves of steel. The orchestra board, still decimated, acceded to their demands.

It soon became clear that in the twilight of his career, the Maestro no longer had patience for the kind of interpretive conductorial license he himself had been subjected to for 50 long years. Now ever steady and metronomic, he analyzed his scores exhaustively, meticulously excising any trace of emotional excess. In his hands, the baton possessed a hypnotic precision, truly comforting for those counting the minutes until rehearsal's end, though more than one guest soloist had to be elbowed back into consciousness. He was perhaps not at his best in the more sedate repertoire. One evening, during a performance of the Samuel Barber "Adagio for Strings," he succeeded in mesmerizing even himself and plunged face-first into the score. His life was saved only by grace of his cast-iron facial prosthetic, which splintered the podium table resulting in a career-ending inner ear perforation.

Enrico Splashowski "Per-fec-tion: There Ees No Subs Tit Toot" (2007-2008). When Splashowski burst onto the local scene fresh off the boat from an undisclosed, but culturally rich former Soviet bloc country, this larger-than-life conductor's conductor immediately established a new musical standard. A round-faced fellow with orbital wisps of blondish hair, he terminated half the string section and was able to replace them with a dizzying array of former Moscow Conservatory classmates flown in with vague promises of remuneration and Rocky Mountain polygamy. Naturally, his popularity among the original indigenous musicians declined, but upon realizing they'd been duped, East European cronies were fairly more critical. Splashowski uttered his famous quote backstage after compatriots presented him with a large, inadequately iced Black Sea crab, the meal that ended at Slope Community Medical Center Hospice Care.

Climax: 2008-The Present

After centuries of excellence, the untimely death of Maestro Splashowski, and becoming nearly bankrupt, the Orchestra Board was poised to find a conductor who would usher them into the 21st century. No longer able to afford any of the reputable soloists capable of holding an audience's interest, the Board resolved to search the land for a native English speaker capable of charming the spouses of older, more affluent potential donors. The advent and artistic directorship of new Maestro Michel Butrie, DMA, carries with it any number of firsts: the first African-American orchestra member (DeJonte Jones, triangle/utility bongo), the first tenured woman orchestra member (Harleen Marie, Principal Viola), and, of course, the nation's first bovine concertmaster. Today, the Stonehaven Symphony boasts a repertoire that spans from the masterworks of deceased Caucasians to deft orchestral transcriptions of the latest smooth jazz. The ensemble's quota of nubile young Asian string players is comparable to that of many of the region's finest community orchestras.

In a recent Colorado Public Radio interview, Maestro Michel Butrie, DMA was asked to sum up the future of the orchestra, or at least his own career prospects, within the broader context of his predecessor's demise. Taking a deep breath, he glanced furtively to either side, then whispered: "Excellence is its own reward."

MISTRESS TO THE MUSIC

Unknown Staffer

Newspaper Clipping,

Ink on paper

c. 2011

Founded in 1833, the Eastern Slope Pioneer Gazette was one of the longest-running newspapers in the Rocky Mountain region. This faded press clipping was recovered from the Stonehaven Symphony tour bus cargo compartment. You can read an interview with Greta Rimwald nee Vásárhelyi, a Hungarian immigrant who rose to the position of Ladies Guild President. Here she tells the story of her rivalry with outgoing President Suzie Eckstein, a forbidden affair with music director Sandor Vegh, and the 2001 Stonehaven Symphony Dog Wash fundraiser.

Mistress to the Music: Past Symphony Guild President reflects on 60th Anniversary

Sixty years. It is a notable number by any stretch. Many symphony orchestras haven't lasted 60 years. Only in the past half century has human life expectancy reached past the sixth decade. If a marriage between a man and a woman spans that duration, it's cause for a Diamond Anniversary celebration. A 60-year-old dog would be unimaginable.

This year, the Ladies Guild of the Stonehaven Symphony celebrates its 60th year of serving the community and the symphony through grass-roots support, education, and fundraising efforts. The story of the Ladies Guild and how it came to reach this milestone is best told by those who have served and led the organization. Through the decades these older women, from different backgrounds and circumstances, more often than not former trophy wives from unhappy marriages, have committed what is left of their lives to spreading the joy of music. As the arts group prepares to celebrate its Diamond Jubilee Anniversary gala this weekend, one woman who served as Guild President for almost 12 years sat down with the *Eastern Slope Pioneer Gazette* to share her memories.

Greta Rimwald: Stonehaven Symphony Guild President, 2001-2012

Greta Rimwald is an elegantly dressed septuagenarian with coiffed white hair, a stern demeanor, and peeking out from under her pearl necklace, a little baton tattoo. Greta agreed to come to the *Pioneer Gazette* offices for this interview on the condition she be accompanied by her two French bulldogs, Wolfgang and Stone Cold, gifted to her husband by the Stonehaven Dumb Friends League. Their names show Greta's love of classical music and American professional wrestling. Spirited but small-bowelled, one immediately relieved itself behind this reporter's desk.

"Martin, he refuse to be left at the home with these ones anymore. He will not like Wolfgang on his wheelchair doing the humping thing," she says patting the big one's head.

When asked to comment upon the Ladies Guild Fundraiser of '01, Greta wistfully strokes her pearls.

"I think we did not have the fear," she says, "We did not know what we couldn't do, so we did it."

When Greta joined the Guild in 1971, she was relatively new to the Colorado scene. A transplant from Hungary, she brought with her many colorful Hungarian expressions that she has become known for. Green card in hand, she arrived in Slope on the arm of Martin Rimwald, a distinguished, but corpulent local politician.

Of the fairytale romance, she says, "Don't look at the tooth of a gift horse."

Greta had grown up listening to the magnificent orchestras of her native Budapest, so that September her therapist introduced her to the Stonehaven Symphony. Sure enough, she found herself intrigued by the Americans, particularly the next generation of outstanding musician interns from local high schools.

"I always had the *bekapcsol* for these young horn players," Greta remembers. "There is something about the way they prance about on the stage, so free and wild. And you know, the Maestro was so hot. All the Guild Girls thought so."

In fact, ages of the 16 Guild "Girls" ranged from their late-50s to mid-80s, many former mail-order brides from Soviet bloc countries that no longer exist. It was mentioned that if math serves, Greta herself must have been nearly 70 years old when Maestro Zoltan Vegh was forced to step down under a cloud of improprieties in 2007. There were rumors of inappropriate relationships with Stonehaven Symphony staff and board members.

"Foolish wind blows out of a foolish hole," Greta snaps. "I remember his smooth tongue in my ear like it was yesterday."

When asked how Mr. Rimwald felt about her obvious affection for the maestro, Greta says, "That old *gyik* ? He says musicians are not men, how do you say, in the sexual sense. But Martin doesn't think the professional wrestling is real either."

"In those days, membership cost $1. There were many of the good-looking young musicians, and we girls did everything by hand," Greta says.

The Ladies Guild would primp up in their old fishnet stockings and torpedo bras, then visit local high schools Friday mornings before each concert. The ladies would typically turn down the lights in the classroom and play classical recordings. Sometimes, they would incorporate movement with terrified male students: dance steps or historical dances such as the Gavotte, Cha Cha, and Bunga Bunga. Female students were evidently left somewhere else with a box of old symphony brochures. There was no publicity, funding, or reprisals for this unique brand of musical exposure. The Ladies Guild did it because they cared deeply. "Even if we only reach one of those boys, we have done our job. We got them interested in something they had no clue about," she adds with a wink.

But by 2000, the orchestra was in trouble. Ticket sales were down. Players were taking better-paying jobs. Maestro Vegh threatened to kill himself and the horn section. Suzie Eckstein née Dragojlov, Acting Ladies Guild President, May-August, 2001, convened an emergency meeting. "That Suzie," Greta says, "she was, how do you say, a 'wooden bitch.'" As Acting President, Eckstein had frowned upon Greta's school presentations. It also concerned Greta that at a time when Zoltan Vegh was separated from his wife, Eckstein used her position at to justify one-on-one meetings with the maestro, to which she showed up "dressed like an old catfish." Evidently, Eckstein was known to share intimate details at the meetings afterwards, whispering to a rapt audience with a sly Yugoslav accent. She told them all how the great man had clung to her and wept freely as he confided that Mrs. Vegh could no longer endure his emotional neediness and narcissism. Though none of the Ladies Guild had ever met his wife, the consensus was that she must be a witch.

Greta explains that Eckstein always interrupted Guild functions to talk on her cellphone. During the emergency meeting, she received a call from daughter who was teaching at a local Hebrew school. They spent five minutes talking about a car wash fundraiser the school was hosting. When she got off the phone, Suzie suggested the Ladies Guild try a car wash fundraiser for the Symphony. Greta had been very annoyed. When asked if there might have been just a little rivalry between them, Greta snaps, "Yes, well, the fence is not made from sausage! I said. Nobody does the car washes in Budapest. Dog wash is better!"

Many of the Ladies Guild were dog lovers. One had a teenaged grandson who was involved with community service at the Dumb Friends League, as was the case for many convicted juveniles. In fact, many child offenders doing community service there had been traumatized by the Ladies Guild school presentations just a few years prior. Suzie Eckstein insisted the maestro would never agree to put on a Symphony dog wash, but Greta was determined to invite him to the following Monday night Ladies Guild meeting because she steadfastly believed there was a way to do it. "And we Guild girls knew what to do with the men," says Greta.

That Monday evening, they were all abuzz and barely able to get through the luncheon arrangements on the agenda. Greta remembers when Maestro Vegh had finally appeared and how they had excitedly ushered him to a vacant chair at the head of the table where he was breathlessly questioned. They asked him about the latest ticket sales and the orchestra debt. How were things with Mrs. Vegh, they asked, and did he need a place to spend the night? He had shaken his head until he finally stood up and stammered that yes, finances were dire, but the idea of respectable musicians washing dogs was degrading. Then, tears filled his eyes as he recalled that the week before their separation, his wife had purchased a hairless Chinese Crested purebred without his consent and named it Adolph. It had been the topic of their last argument.

The Ladies Guild was furious that this woman could be so insensitive. Besides, it was unthinkable to buy a dog from a breeder with so many shelter animals waiting for adoption, "waiting for the forever home," Greta says. Overcome by the memory, the maestro collapsed in his chair, sobbing amidst the Ladies' hisses of "Burn the witch!"

Slope has a well-known stray dog problem. Mongrels have roamed our downtown streets at night for years, scaring children and impregnating female species. As part of their court-mandated community service, a group of teenaged volunteers from the Dumb Friends League had attended a city council meeting that spring and demanded funding for expanded spay-and-neuter services. Greta's husband Martin, then city council president, had cautiously applauded their initiative, noting how important it is to empower the at-risk teens of the future, many of whom had only been convicted of driving-related offences. But the council had also been under considerable pressure from Ed Eckstein, Suzie's husband. Ed Eckstein was one of the wealthiest men in Eastern Slope and a major donor to various causes, including Martin Rimwald's own doomed mayoral campaign. Eckstein also ran the local Jewish Political Action Committee (JPAC), an ultra-Orthodox organization that opposes the neutering of animals. The teenagers' application was denied.

The entire Ladies Guild showed up with coffee and cookies at the next orchestra rehearsal. As Acting President, Suzie Eckstein was obligated to present Greta's Symphony Dog Wash Fundraiser idea to the musicians. Maestro Vegh had hushed the orchestra, then quickly excused himself from the stage. He had evidently assumed, as did Suzie Eckstein herself, that the orchestra would be outraged. The presentation was not well-received.

"That Suzie was scolded like the pig bought for a *pengő*," Greta laughs. Several of the musicians threatened to resign on the spot. Two senior orchestra members fainted, but Greta had also taken the liberty of inviting the outgoing Symphony treasurer, Bill Lighthead. Bill's report was brief, but ominous: the entire Stonehaven Symphony was on the verge of bankruptcy, and the orchestra would likely soon be unemployed unless drastic measures were undertaken.

The next Saturday morning, dozens of musicians solemnly lined up outside Slope Auditorium with old towels and wash buckets.

"You should have seen the sweaty little faces," Greta laughs. "They look like they have the stake in their ass!"

The Ladies Guild purchased dog shampoo in bulk and borrowed hoses. They set out water bowls for dogs that would be waiting in the queue and bottled refreshments for their owners. Greta says that while Suzie Eckstein paced back and forth behind the loading dock making furtive phone calls, a small crowd of curious season subscribers gathered in front of the Slope Auditorium. Most didn't even bring pets. They watched volunteers unload boxes of the promotional Stonehaven Symphony t-shirts Greta had ordered.

"And there was also Martin," Greta sighs. "Parking in our Mercedes behind the dumpster again."

In fact, four months prior, Martin Rimwald had begun to receive anonymous phone calls. A whispery female voice with a strong accent would describe Greta's interactions with young male orchestra musicians in often graphic detail. Since that time, Martin could often be spotted at orchestra rehearsals, behind music stands, or under tables. That Saturday, he arrived just in time to see the Dumb Friends League pull up in a truck. It was an old yellow Chevy Silverado they had converted into a fully functioning mobile clinic and covered with what Greta recalls was an illegible homemade banner promoting their big upcoming spay-neuter event. When he saw what they had done, Martin pried himself out of his car and angrily made his way over to the laughing teenagers. Dumb Friends Director Marc Sendler tried to defuse the situation, explaining that a neighborhood dispensary had sponsored the whole project. He repeated how important it was to empower the at-risk youth of tomorrow. Pulling aside the offending banner, they offered Martin a tour of the interior.

"He could not believe his eye holes!" Greta exclaims.

It certainly could not have been easy for the high school dropouts to weld together the primitive surgery table, laryngoscope, and an active gas evac system for neutering female dogs. He had never seen an anesthesia machine built out of old cannabis extractor parts. An animal net and veterinary dart gun were mounted behind the driver's seat for effect. But the old vending truck still smelled like food, possibly fish.

Outside the truck, Greta and Suzie had been arguing about a mistake in the t-shirt order. "I tell them I want to pay a small price for shirts. They sent me the small shirts," Greta says. "Ass heads!"

The shirts had represented quite an investment on the part of the Ladies Guild. It hadn't been easy for Greta to find the unbelievably low price through a Vietnamese distributor. Though in retrospect and considering how little fabric is necessary for an Asian size small, the price made sense. She also saved money using as few colors and letters as possible, using acronyms wherever she could. Untenured members of the orchestra had set modesty aside and squeezed into their shirts before returning to the dog wash queue though so few pets had been volunteered, a number of strays had to be gathered up instead. A number had been partially tranquilized by teenagers who had gotten their hands on the Dumb Friends' veterinary dart rifles and were firing at will.

While Martin was inside the truck, Zoltan Vegh arrived. The maestro stated that he'd just received an anonymous phone call from a whispering female informant telling him the fundraiser was being held despite his objections. Fighting back tears, he then held out the little dog he had just been awarded in the divorce settlement. The Ladies Guild immediately dropped whatever animals they had in hand and flocked around him. He was surrounded by a half-dozen elderly women. They were soaking wet and wearing t-shirts that frankly left little to the imagination. But the ladies were less affectionate toward his ex-wife's hairless surrogate. Greta herself had taken one look at the creature, then back at the deep frothy trough she had stepped away from.

"I picked up Adolph, and I said, 'The accidents happen.'"

She was about to give Adolph "the last bath of his life" when Martin emerged. Suzie Eckstein had rushed over to meet him.

"Now he was saying that they were good kids and he liked the truck. He asked them what kind of food he smelled. He thought maybe pickled fish," Greta remembers. "But he said they must take down the words."

Before the teenagers had a chance to protest, she saw Suzie smile and point down the street.

"There, behind God's back, you could see a parade."

There at the bottom of the street leading up to the auditorium were big placards, Klezmer music, and a group of 12-16 men in prayer shawls. They held up big pictures of scissors and frightened animals bearing the JPAC logo. "Castration is a sin," read one sign. Another read "If an animal has bruised, crushed, torn, or cut sex glands, you must not offer it to the LORD."

They were marching toward Slope Auditorium.

"When I saw that look on Martin's face, I knew," says Greta. "The monkey will now jump in the water."

In a shrill voice some present said they had never heard a mayoral candidate use, he screamed at the kids. He begged them to take down their banner. Martin Rimwald was a large man, some might say morbidly obese. As the marchers came up hill, he ambled over to the side of the mobile clinic and tried to pull down the fabric with his sheer girth.

Greta remembers that the Jewish Political Action Committee seemed surprised to see a half-dozen elderly women with the letters "SS" plastered on their chests flanking a 300-pound man swinging from an enormous "Bitch-A-Thon" banner.

Greta prefers to see the glass as half-full. "After all, it was not like any of the marchers could read English," she remembers. "But the picture of Martin in the newspaper was not good."

In fact, the men couldn't read English. The men weren't even really Jewish; they were Hispanic laborers Ed Eckstein had hired to fill in for Jewish students who normally would have been called upon to demonstrate. Local rabbis had told him yeshiva boys shouldn't come out for the spay-neuter protest because of what they might be exposed to. It was also true that Eckstein had gone so far as to try dress the men in head-to-toe prayer shawls. There had been so many Mexicans he ran out of shawls. The rest were just wearing ski masks, luchador máscara, and whatever they could get their hands on.

Martin Rimwald did not know the protesters couldn't read English. He also did not know that as the enormous banner slowly ripped in two, the food truck's original signage would be clearly visible. Greta remembered that as her husband slipped to the curb in back of the mobile spay-neuter clinic covered by yards of gaily colored fabric and the bright letters of "Polansky's Kosher Oasis" were revealed for all to see.

Evidently, Martin had desperately glanced from the truck to the marchers and screamed, "Get outta here! Drive, drive!"

One of the teenagers leapt behind the steering wheel and started the old truck up in a plume of dark exhaust fumes. The Mexicans were unable to understand what Martin was saying, but they could see that the big man was lying on the curb behind the smoking vehicle. They threw down their signs, waved their hands, and rushed to help him. In Martin Rimwald's defense, the sight of the Mexican luchadors coming at him out of the smoke must have been deeply disturbing. It was only natural that he would try to fight them off. Two of them wrestled with Martin valiantly as they tried to lift him and move his obese frame out from under the mobile clinic as it suddenly lurched backward. They almost succeeded.

"I think we raised, what, $172?" Greta recalls. "It was the Ladies Guild most successful fundraiser ever. It was more successful than any of that Suzie Eckstein's fundraisers."

When pressed about the invaluable contributions of all the Guild's past presidents, she says, "Well, for sure, without people like Suzie who laid the foundation, we would have had nothing to build the money on. Of course, after the accident the orchestra board made that old walrus resign," she says, stroking Stone Cold's head. "I was torn apart with the laughing. Suzie tried to blame it on me, but everybody, they just took one look at poor Martin and they say we suffered enough already."

Greta had to endure Martin's six months of hospitalization and 16 surgeries, all the while going back and forth between the bedside of a husband who had lost all sensation below the waist and Maestro Zoltan Vegh, who had not. Greta is not in any way embittered by the sacrifices she and countless other Ladies Guild presidents have made over the past 60 years and now celebrate with pride.

"We did not know what we couldn't do, so we did it. We did it for the music," Greta muses. "After all, you can't make the bacon out of a dog."

BACKSTAGE PEEPS

Stonehaven Symphony Front Desk Receptionist Kenan Schucks Digital Blog

c. 2008

By the late 2000s, the Stonehaven Symphony marketing team decided to boost dwindling ticket sales with a novel tack: why not spotlight individual members of the orchestra so audience members can get to know them better? This short-lived experiment gives us a rare glimpse into the musicians' vibrant personalities, not to mention low morale. One by one, musicians Lee Chuk, Mollie Lay, Parker De Von, Harleen Marie, Vera Azaduzi, and DeJonte Jones express their dissatisfaction with orchestral life in general - and one pops concert in particular.

The Blog of Kenan Schucks
Lover of Reggae, Long Walks, Scented Body Paint,
and Receptionist of the Stonehaven Symphony Orchestra

May 2, 2008

Lee Chuk
Principal Cello
Joined the orchestra: 1987

As leader of the cello players and one of only two persons of color in the Stonehaven Symphony, Lee Chuk is very qualified for his current gig as Principal Cello. He says his job is find out what the concertmaster wants and tell the cellos, but for more than 20 years, Lee has also been the wise old Asian mentor in the orchestra. I was tasked with figuring out questions for an interview. It is what it is.

How do Chinese people to learn to play cello?

Lee: Well, Kenan, same way as everyone else. The snow goose doesn't need a bath to be white.

When did you first become interested in music?

Lee: My earliest memory is of my mother singing me to sleep. My mother immigrated to the United States in search of a new life. She moved to Denver, and after she married my father, a kindly philosophy professor from Beijing, they had me. I always had a good ear for music. Every night they would come into my room, and she would sing me a lullaby and kiss me goodnight. Finally, I had to tell her that her voice was not good. After that, she was never the same. When my father was done beating me, the next step was cello lessons.

What is it like to play in the Stonehaven Symphony?

Lee: Interesting question, Kenan. You know, an orchestra with a conductor is like the pieces in a jigsaw puzzle box. Each player in the box is a different shape, each has different colors, with so many different musical ideas. You look at our personal stories one at a time, musicians who learned how to play all over the world, people from every walk of life, it's amazing we can even play together! But do you know the one thing we do have in common?

What?

Lee: At the end of the day, we're still in a box.

What is special to you about the Stonehaven Symphony Pops Concert Series?

Lee: Obviously, ticket sales are important. I understand why management feels the need to bring in popular musicians. The audience here doesn't have the attention span to sit through Mozart and Beethoven every week. They seem to like loud amplification, big stage shows, the video wall. Pop songs sell. Of course, last month when Li'l Skank overdosed and passed out on stage, paramedics had to shut the whole thing down.

What would you say to young people who aren't sure if they want to play in an orchestra?

Lee: Even the flightless songbird does more than a sleeping eagle.

April 13, 2008

Mollie Lay
Principal Second Violin
Joined the orchestra: 2003

It's not easy to explain why there are second violins in an orchestra. There already is a first violin section. It's even harder to explain Principal Second Violin Mollie Lay, but the symphony held blind auditions and she got the gig fair and square. I'm not judging, but Mollie has more tattoos and body piercings than many African people. Personnel Manager Yup Michaels says she is a walking dress code violation. Here's what I Googled: "The first chair second violin is the "principal second" and gets paid less than the concertmaster but more than a section player."

Why do you get paid more than a section player?

Mollie: Pretty tacky, Kenan! Listen, we all showed up at the audition for the same chair. I just messed up less. There's a lot of competition, it's a jungle out there. But now I'm boojy rich!!

How did you first become interested in music?

Mollie: Did you hear the part about all the money I'm making? Listen, I grew up in Greeley. It's a tough neighborhood. Daddy was a pimp. Mom played clarinet. Daddy told her to stop. Mom hit him. Hard. I was ten years old standing across the porch, and I could taste the blood in my mouth. What was the question?

How did you first become interested in music?

Mollie: Afterward with Daddy at the dentist's, they had a clown that played the violin. Real tall and bald with a beard and creepy fingers. He could pluck the notes to "Humoresque" with his teeth. He made me think evil thoughts! Anyway, Daddy begged him to stop. I asked if he did lessons. Come to find out, Screechy the Clown was once a famous concertmaster. For many years, he led the string section with joy and aplomb. Then, one day they told him he sucked. Told him he messed up too much and fired him. He spent six months losing his mind and cooking meth in the bushes by the Symphony office. Next thing you know, he was a professional therapy clown. Lessons were cool. I can still play "Humoresque" with my mouth!

What is it like to play in the Stonehaven Symphony?

Mollie: Well, distracting. Michel, our conductor, is, in some ways, finger-lickin' good. You know what I'm saying? People give him a hard time. Li'l Skank was gonna ride him like a pony!! But he deserves better. He deserves a good woman who could make a baby daddy out of him. Just wish he'd stop trying to conduct.

What is special to you about the Stonehaven Symphony Pops Concert Series?

Mollie: Pops concerts suck. But I can tell you what was special about last weekend: stage diving. That Skank boi's hardcore! After the thing with his blow-up car, kids in front started throwing finger food. Skank took a pineapple skewer to the crotch! He was vexed. But when he got up on that riser, I didn't know if the Ladies Guild in the front row was gonna catch him. I mean, when a black man suddenly comes out of the air at you like that, you better have two hands on your purse. At least they rolled him back on the stage afterwards. Then, he crawls over to his DJ and in between songs he's still moaning, "Damn, m'leg's busted." It was hilarious. But that DJ was kind of a scumbag. Gives him the White Lollipop, told him to man up. They had bills to pay.

Do you have any words of advice for young people who want to play in an orchestra?

Mollie: Dunno. Don't crush on your conductor. Pops concerts and meth don't go together. Don't quit your day job.

April 11, 2008

Parker DeVon
Utility Horn
Joined the orchestra: 1997

Google says "Some orchestras add the phrase "Utility Horn" to the player's contract to anticipate a situation of having to move players around in a section due to illness." I guess Stonehaven Symphony Utility Horn Parker DeVon just goes with the flow. This might not be that exciting, but he is also supposed to be the Musicians Representative on the Symphony Board.

What does a Symphony board even do?

Parker: We have three responsibilities: overall governance, advocacy for the institution, and fundraising. When the orchestra unanimously selected me in 1998, I was assigned to the Miscellaneous Advisory Sub-Committee. We were charged with assisting Maestro Butrie in the development of an educational program for the Mountain Vista Women's Correctional Facility. We also crafted a public statement in response to the brutal bush beating of a young African-American in the landscaping outside Symphony offices last year.

How did you first become interested in music?

Parker: My mother was a brass section captain during the famous Loveland Cadet Band Steroid Scandal of '62. After the court martial, her black nickel Sterling lay dormant for years. One day while collecting the trash, I found it under a box in the garage. Initially, I thought it was a mangled exhaust pipe and took it out to the curb. When my mother finished beating me, I discovered she was right—you put your mouth on it, buzz your lips, and it makes a sound.

What is it like to play in the Stonehaven Symphony?

Parker: Very rewarding. I get to buzz my lips for a living. Of course, I would never quit my day job at Ball Aerospace. But the other musicians are fascinating. There are brass, wind, percussion, and string instruments. They often play practical jokes. One time I went to play a solo, but the mouthpiece tasted soapy, and my horn blew bubbles. Then there was the time they unanimously elected me to the orchestra board. Ha ha. They say I am like a machine.

What is special to you about the Stonehaven Symphony Pops Concert Series?

Parker: There's not much for a utility horn to do, which is why I like to bring my Kindle to the green room. Almost all the way through my Popular Mechanics subscription now. We have brought in some interesting musicians. A bluegrass musician, jazz, a Peruvian nose flautist. Given our country's history of lynchings, the board also wanted to engage a young African-American individual. We didn't know what

Mumble Rap was. I have no idea why the inflatable Lamborghini made that popping sound and started to collapse after Little Skank crawled inside. Also, his flying drone cameras were ill-advised. When the helium started blowing out of the hole and the bottom part of the float was whipping back and forth, one of the drones clipped its tether and crash-landed in the brass section. Our Principal Tuba lost a lot of blood that night. But it wasn't a real Lamborghini, so I was surprised when it dragged Little Skank all the way across the stage and through the DJ rig.

Do you have any words of advice for young people who want to play in an orchestra?

Parker: Helmets are available at many sporting goods outlets.

April 6, 2008

Harleen Marie
Principal Viola
Joined the orchestra: 1988

Harleen. But don't let her name freak you out: under Principal Viola Harleen Marie's scary looks, she has a heart of gold. When she first played her audition for the orchestra 47 years ago, she didn't wear any shoes. She also didn't have a mustache then. She was like an innocent flower child. To be honest, playing in an orchestra for 47 years changed her. Now she is definitely a person of few words. Those words may be hurtful at times.

Is it true that you auditioned barefoot?

Harleen: Who said that?

He made me promise not to tell.

Harleen: Lee! This is the kind of patriarchal cesspool I have to work in.

How did you first become interested in music?

Harleen: Interested in music? What kind of professional musician is interested in music? I'm interested in maintaining a high standard in my section. I'm interested in doing things well or not doing them at all. Can you say that about yourself?

Nope. Is that why Vera says you're always sick when there's a viola solo?

Harleen: What?

What is it like to play in the Stonehaven Symphony?

Harleen: It's more pleasant than this interview. The musicians are not stupid. They know that if they want to get paid, they have to play in tune. This is not to say that there isn't some dead wood back there, in the back of the viola section. When I hear a note that's out of tune, I'll immediately go back there. I don't like to go back there, but I do. It smells funny. It smells like old musician back there. I don't even know their names. None of them will meet my eyes. I say, if you tell me who played out of tune, nobody will get fired.

What is special to you about the Stonehaven Symphony Pops Concert Series?

Harleen: That's a tough one. Everybody knows pops concerts aren't real music. We get incredibly dumbed down, simple parts. All we do is make background musical wallpaper behind the guest artists. Most of these pop stars have no idea how an orchestra works and they don't care. Like that Li'l Skank guy. Before the concert, his crew brought in helium tanks and filled up these stupid inflatable floats and they took up most of the stage. One was the Korean sex doll, just gross. There was the 10-foot tall working hookah pipe. And the car, tethered literally right against the side of the viola section. Some people couldn't even see Michel's hands because the thing was in the way. Li'l Skank makes his big entrance, and his mic stand is right by me, I don't even have enough room to bow. Then, he grabs the front of the car and starts dancing and grinding his pelvis into it. It was bumping into our music stand over and over. I had to get away. We don't get paid enough for this, and we hardly get paid. But that's when my bow got stuck. The tip went right into the rubber. I really didn't know what to do. Tried to slowly pull the wood out, then it made this terrible rubbery squeaking noise, so I stopped. But the big car balloon was obviously leaking air. Finally, I decided to just rip it.

Do you have any words of advice for young people who want to play in an orchestra?

Harleen: "Why." That's a word. Or "don't." Don't bother unless you're willing to really practice and play in-tune. And use deodorant.

April 4, 2008

Vera Azaduzi
Section First Violin
Joined the orchestra: 2005

Vera Azuduzi is like the inner child of the First Violin Section. You can feel her positive energy. Vera says she just graduated from the Musicescu Music Academy, which is in one of the East European countries. I think it's got "mold" in the name. Moldivia? Moldakstahn? She says it's famous for classical music.

How did you first become interested in music?

Vera: Well, I loved this violin since as long as I can remember. I always wanted to have one. When I was little girl in Moldova, they had cartoon with the little sheep trying to play violin. I thought it was the cutest thing, that little sheep with all the other farm animals, trying to make music. It was so funny, you know. It wasn't until I come here to Slope that Harleen tell me that the violin strings come from inside the sheep that are dead.

What is it like to play in the Stonehaven Symphony?

Vera: For me it is like dream come true! I am so happy! You are in the middle of the other musicians that you don't even know, you are not able to hear the sound what you are playing. And the musicians are so, so special. I don't remember who the concertmaster is this week, but Mollie is really, really interesting! And Harleen is my hero! She never complains or asks anything for herself, but Lee told me she is very sick woman! Lee told me that she has the face cancer! But at last night's rehearsal with Mr. Skunk, she was so brave. She continued to play until the big viola solo. You know that solo, in the "Overture to Biotch Needs It Bad"? She started coughing and I thought she would die! Thank God for that college boy sitting beside Harleen! He played her solo, no problem. Just like what happened at the concert we had last month!

What is special to you about the Stonehaven Symphony Pops Concert Series?

Vera: Oh, is very special, you know. So much American Pop music that we won't have back in Moldova. I never heard a banjo before. What a funny little instrument! Is it supposed to make the plinking sound? And I never seen the black people doing the rapping before, only DeJonte. Mr. Skunk has the funny hair, and he has gold in his teeth. I think he maybe looks like a pirate who fell off a boat in Africa! But he seemed a little sad. Maybe he couldn't find belt for his droopy pants? I don't think he liked the piccolo solo we made. You know that solo, in the "Twerk My Rod"? He talked to his friend with the record players. He told his friend that our orchestra music sounds like dead people! But Mr. Skunk was very friendly. He also invited me and Juli up to his hotel room. He said he wanted me and Juli to show him what is a sextuplet. He didn't know! Well, I didn't know what is *ganja*. I sure do now!

Did you and Juli sleep with Li'l Skank?

Vera: There was already some person in his bed! I think they were dead. It looked like DeJonte.

Do you have any words of advice for young people interested in doing your kind of work?

Vera: You will have so special experience! Remember 911 on the phone. Well, after *ganja*, you are going to get the munchies. Don't worry, is normal, you know. And buy loud alarm clock!

April 1, 2008

DeJonte Jones
Principal Triangle and Utility Bongo
Joined the orchestra: 2006

When Black people first arrived on our shores, a lot of people questioned whether they could ever fit in with symphonies. Since that time, there have been many famous Black people: Martin Luther King. LeBron James. I'm sure there are others I'm not mindful of. From his grounded beginnings, probably as a sharecropper's son, to playing in a symphony orchestra, Principal Triangle and Utility Bongo DeJonte Jones has seen a lot of stereotypes every step of the way.

What was it like to grow up on a plantation?

DeJonte: Plantation, mah ass, Dawg, you an' me went to da same high skoo. Loveland High Skoo! You's in mah motha fuckin' health class! 'Member Human Sexuality? You fainted!

How did you first become interested in music?

DeJonte: Well, growin' up, Pops always playin' us. He find like a Taiwan nose flute song an' crank it up just to piss off Uncle Jermaine. Then mah damn uncle would come back wid a record of sum Alpine Yodelin' an' blow Pops' mind! Momma had to leave da crib. One day, I foun' this old mix tape of Ludwig van Mothafucka Beethoven at Walmart. "Meeresstille und Glückliche Fahrt." Stupidest damn thin' I evah heard. Got this big-ass timpani drum right at da end. I brought it home an' cranked it up. Mah mothafucka Pops an' Jermaine looked at each other. They re-evaluate their life!

Okay. What is it like to play in the Stonehaven Symphony?

DeJonte: A'ight. My boys in the percussion section, we chill. Sometimes too much. I mean, most of da time we ain't do sheiit. We jus' counting the rests 'fore we're s'pposed to play. Just like Parker. Fool spend most of his time fappin' in da green room. Now me, I be checkin' out the shorties. There sure be some fine wimmin hereabouts! But I dunno where Mollie got da big-ass lip plate. Look like something outta National Mothafucka Geographic. When we do play, we usually too loud. Harleen look at us like we're crazy loud, but in like a hundred years, nobody never heards that viola make a damn sound! An' that Lee Chuk nigga, he real subtle-like. When we be bangin', he tell the maestro mebbe he should put his 'cello down an' go out an' listen to da balance. 'Cuz sometimes Massa, he forget about us. Then, booyow, my boys usually get a bunch of notes at da end! Who's that thick hottie who sit near us in da back, Vera? Oooh, she be smilin' and movin' and gettin' down to our beats! Sometimes I just start grinnin' and think if I really set my boys free and we get to bangin', we'd jus' burn the orchestra down!

What is special to you about the Stonehaven Symphony Pops Concert Series?

DeJonte: Smokin' crack wid Li'l Skank at da hotel. Man, though. dat wuz some strong sheiit! Just wish I be in any condition to play da show - I done passed out in his bed. Dreamed I was a clown, choo dig? Staring at muh mothafucka face in the mirror. Starin' at da fakey, flakey white make-up peelin' off mah mothafucka face, an' I see the black underneath. Startin' to wondah what am I doin' here? Who am I playin'? It was bad! But then, choo know, I woke up there in Slope Community Medical. An' as I'm comin' 'round, everythin's blurry. There's doctors an' nurses… an' there's dis tall skinny bald nigga. He playin' violin wid his teeth! I'm like, what 'chew thinkin', Man?

Do you have any words of advice for young people interested in doing your kind of work?

DeJonte: Bro! Stay away from clowns.

STAR-CROSS'D

Screenshots, Mobile SMS

c. 2008

The job of an orchestral personnel manager is a thankless one. Stonehaven Symphony Personnel Manager Yup Michael's was much the same. While official accounts of the 2008 Romeo and Juliet Ballet Debacle suggest dancers on stage were to blame, recovered text exchanges between members of the pit orchestra during performances leading up to the fateful night tell a different story.

With actual cellphone screengrabs, we can watch while, despite Yup's best efforts, a feud develops between the violinists and violists even as true love blossoms between two musicians, a tragedy of Shakespearean proportions!

(Group MMS)

Text Message
Tuesday, Apr 15, 8:39 AM

Yup

> This is a reminder for all participating Stonehaven Symphony Orchestra musicians that start time for Prokofiev Romeo and Juliet is 7:30 PM tomorrow evening at Stonehaven Auditorium. Dress is all black for men and women. Park at the West Lot.

> Maestro Michel Butrie has again requested that all electronic devices be switched off for the complete duration of the performance.

Ty

Wednesday, Apr 16, 7:39 PM

> hey benni
> what's the difference between a violin and a diaper

> Couldn't care less, Ty. Entrance coming up.

> a diaper has an ass on the inside

> . . . .

who da man ???

. . . .

Wednesday 7:41 PM

ouch girl !!!

Dammit. Now you must be so proud.

oooh benni violins kinda choked on that high note

You only dream of playing a note that high, viola boy.
You only dream of playing intelligible pitches.

yeah violas don't have that squeaky crap

How do you save a choking violist?

oooh benni the jokester ???

Take your foot off his neck.

that's all u got

Hold up. We got another one coming…

an entrance or a joke ?

....

that's all u got benni

your violin squeaks
you don't like men
you got no reason to live

> That was close.
> Now Michel's doing the Zorro thing with his baton.
> And he's always got his pouty deer in the headlights look
> even when he's looking right at you.
> Wait. Ty?
> That's your cue!.

....

Wednesday, 7:44 PM

> Ty you guys totally missed it. And he caught you with your phone. You are so busted.

....

> Who da man now

Benni

Wednesday, Apr 16, 11:49 PM

> oh snap. did ty get fired?

> Don't be such a drama queen, Ramon. He just got probation. Had to meet with Michel. Bet he got a butt full.

> jesus. but honestly i did not notice. was watching the hawt dancers. xoxoxo.

> When that douchebag missed the cue, he totally messed up the violas. Dragon Lady missed her viola solo, you should have seen that scowly look of hers. Though Harleen always has the same basic look. Ramon, how could you not notice? Ty just ruined the whole ballet all by hisself.

> lucky you were texting him at the time.

> Ty tried to mess with me. I then played him like a cheap violin.

> he is lucky he didn't lose the gig. you are lucky you didn't lose the gig. you guys are messed up.

> Ramon! What's up with you?

>								no thing
> it's all just messed up
> where did all this hating begin?

Ty started it.

>								all the jokes.

Come on! Violists like Ty started off playing the violin and they suck. Then they switch to viola because the notes are easier. Now they sit right beside us getting paid as much as we do. Rehearsals are boring enough as is. Hating them is what we do.

> i used to do viola, it was kinda meh. some violists are okay. What about roslyn.?

Ros again! You horny toad! She's got good fingers, but I'm telling you, she likes girls. You'll never get anywhere.

> i must try. You see her in her shorts last night? she is hawt.

She is gay.

>								no

I got a better chance than you do.
Just don't want you get hurt, Chihuahua.

> you are too late she has already pierced my heart.
> i must talk with her.

Well then you ask her. Say "Did you like Benni's halter top last Tuesday?"

> that was no halter top. it was leather bra.

Whatever. You ask her. The bra never lies.

Ramon

Thursday, Apr 17, 11:19 AM

So

> So? What happened with Ros?

so unfortunately the bra speaks the truth.

> I'm so sorry, Ramon!
> Tell Aunt Benni everything.

so I went over to the viola side during break.

> Stop. Right. There. You went over to the viola side? Were you stoned?

how else can I meet her? it was not that bad.

> Where was Ty? Was he there?

yes. he made many jokes. he told the one about violinists and dog whistles but I would not listen.

> He's a douchebag.

rosalyn listened. she laughed long and hard. she has her sexy laugh.

> No she didn't. Really? Did she?

they all laughed.

> Hoes!

they all laughed. all of them except the new girl.

> New girl?

juli from oberlin.

> Spooky emo?

yes juli. she was at oberlin when I was there.

Obie skank!

no. she actually stood up for me. she said if ty told what people like about the violinists and dog whistles, he should also tell what people like about violists and christmas lights.

To hang them on trees?.

she knew that one. she is different than the rest. like a dark confused flower. this is her first big gig. she is kind of depressed about it. we talked a long time.

Got it. Here's what I think. I think she wants your big gig.

no benni. juli is different.
and so hawt.

I thought you said she was different.

i must know her. will you help me? i need your help.

Straight guys always needing the help.
Keeps the population under control.

juli from oberlin.

Spooky emo?

yes juli. she was at oberlin when I was there.

Obie skank!

Juli

Thursday, Apr 17, 1:45 PM

Harleen! Hope I got your number right. Texting in traffic! Tell me all about that Ramon right now!!

....

Hey, is your phone crapping out again? Did you see his pecs in that tank top? ;) Looks like he never practiced a day in his life. Tell me he's not gay.

um you have dialed the wrong number

GR8 I'm late! Can you believe the speed limit's only 65. But I got your texts, Harles, this number's working fine. But what do you think of Ramon? PLZ! Wait a sec, I gotta gun it past this jerk....

So what's Ramon's story? Is there a GF? It's so hard to find a real man in this orchestra. Orchestra men are just so common, you know. Vera tried to set me up with Crowley. That dude smokes more than me. But did you see, Ramon was so brave to come over to the viola side. I was talking to Roz and Marko tried to stop him, but he came right up. With that mucho accent of his, and his he-man stubble on his face. Maybe there's something wrong with him, you know my luck with guys. I promised my therapist I wouldn't do any more violin players and here I go again. But he's into me, Harles, he was so smooth, did you see him take my phone and put his number in? His fingers were still shaking, though, just like an audition. And I saw his eyes just kept going down my tee. Bet he's just a cuddly he- hunk! Well what do you think????

um juli you texted that number i did put in your phone

What do you mean? Yup gave me your number last week.

....

Oh. God. Ramon?

Lee

Friday, Apr 18, 1:59 AM

> hey man guess who is in juli simpson's bathroom

> Ramon. What time is it?

> i am sorry but it is kind of urgent.

> Here is a hint: it's 2 am.

> you are right. your wisdom as principal cello player has much respect through the stonehaven symphony.that is why i need your advice.

> Sleep you need sleep. Go back to sleep.

> I cannot. juli waits for me now. she waits for her bebe. That is what she calls me now.

> Juli the spooky emo?

> oh yes. it has been quite the night. we went out to the movie theater. she showed much emotion.

> How much emotion did she show?

> i am here in her bathroom at 2 am.

OK well done. Where is she?

> in her bed. the bed we have shared for three hours.

Bravo. My work here is done good night.

> but what do i say to her now? what should i do?

Sounds to me like you know exactly what to do.

> lee she now says she cannot live without me. we have only been out together tonight. it is freaking me.

True she is a violist. You are of the violin clan. This will not end well.

> i do not want it to end well. i do not want it to end. she is hawt.

Yes well Ramon snap out of it.

> but i feel love.

Love. So rare in our orchestra.
It could destroy the delicate balance of hating.

Harleen

Friday, Apr 18, 11:45 PM

OK, Juli. WTF was going on back there with the violins?

I'm so sorry, Harles. The second violins just blew up and it's all my fault.☹

You don't play violin.

But Ty and Marko were fighting because of me. :() I think Marko told Ty that Vera was talking to Mollie about me and Ramon. Ty just couldn't handle it. I don't think the orchestra can handle musicians with deep feelings. Harles, you've always been so real. But maybe this orchestra just isn't doing it for me.

Ty doesn't play violin.

Well, you know the Duel part where the dancer with the big pecs comes out? Ty kept reaching over and flipping Ramon's pages with his bow while he was trying to play. At first I think they were joking about it, but then Ramo missed one of the entrances. Ty just wouldn't quit. I thought Michel or Yup was going to catch them.

What about Marko? He totally lost it.

> Ty kept poking Ramon's music with his bow and he was trying to reach the extension cord on the wall and unplug Ramon's light. He was totally out of control.

So what about Marko?

> Ty accidently ripped out Marko's cord. Right in the middle of the divisi. Then Michel looked right at Marko. Marko couldn't see in the dark, but I guess he felt he had to play something.

Sounded like Pop Goes the Weasel.

> He made it worse with the cursing.

At least it was Bulgarian.

> I don't think anybody in the front row needed a translation.

Well he's fired now.

> OMG. When?

Michel sent Yup over at break. Speaking of cursing, what's the deal with Ty?

> While Ty was busy laughing at Marko, Ramon reached back and hooked the tip of his bow around that top piece of his wire stand. Ty had an entrance coming up. He tried to pull the bow up and splintered the whole tip off. It was a nice bow, too. He couldn't even play the rest of the act. Yup was pissed. He was going on about how as personnel manager, he was going to fire Ty for disruptive whatever. Ty got all croaky. He said he borrowed the bow and that it was worth $10K and he can't afford to get it fixed blah blah. Yup says you're principal viola and he wants to talk to you first. What are you going to tell him?

That was my bow.

Lee

Saturday, Apr 19, 9:06 AM

> Hi Lee Chuk - it's Juli Simpson!

WTF. I've been expecting you.

> Did Ramon talk to you? So I need your advice. Ramon says you're chill and Harleen says you've been at Stonehaven forever. But everybody treats Ramon and me like dirt because of the violin viola thing. Lee, I waited my whole life for a boy like Ramon. Maybe I need to quit the orchestra.

Don't trust Harleen.

> What do you mean? At least she's not fake, like Ty and the rest of the viola section. If it weren't for Harles, I would never have done the viola section. I did violin at Oberlin.

Hmmm. You know now that Ty and Marko are gone, there's a new viola opening and a new violin opening.

> GR8. Now the orchestra has a violin opening. If they'd had a violin audition last month, I would have taken it instead of the viola audition.

Michel wants to have the auditions Saturday. Yup told me hardly anybody signed up and I can go home early.

> OK, wait. It's a blind audition, behind a screen like the last one, right

Yes it is. Nobody knows who's playing the auditions.

> So if I took the violin audition, the audition committee won't know it's me? Or that I'm trying to leave a viola chair.

Correct.

> I still know those violin excerpts! Ramon and I could betogether!! Lee PLEASE tell me you're positive it's a blind audition!!!!

The auditions are blind. Like love.

Harleen

Saturday, Apr 19, 9:45 AM

> Hey Bebe! Did you sleep in after I left? XOXOXOX

Juli? Are you trying to text and drive again?

> Yes Ramon I'm running late and the traffic is gawd awful. Gotta make it back in time to get my old violin from the shop before lunch.

Are you trying to text Ramon?

> Ha ha, Ramon, you're zany with a hangover! But big news: they're holding violin auditions for Marko's chair tonight and I just signed up. I don't want to play stinky old viola wood no more. I just wanna sit next to you and play high screechy notes and cuddle during the rests.

Juli, is that all playing the viola means to you?

> Oh hang on Ramon, pulling up, gotta go, luv u, XOXOXOXO!!!!

Ramon

Saturday, Apr 19, 11:39 AM

hey harleen this is ramon. from the violin section. how are you today?

> No way. Juli Simpson's Ramon?

yes it is so. has juli mentioned me to you?

> ….

i am sorry to bother you but the reason is that i wish to take the viola audition tonight and because you are principal of the violas i seek your advice.

> This is a joke. Right?

no this is no joke. i have studied the viola back in mexico city. i just do not know which excerpts you recommend me to study from the list.

> And you're going to tell me you're doing this so you can sit next to Juli because she's in the viola section.

miss harleen, i have studied the viola back where i come from. I did stop when I was young because of the low notes did affect my stomach but i love her very much and know that I can succeed. please do tell me what should I practice now to do better or do you think I should not do this now?

> Sure. Go ahead, Ramon. Knock yourself out.

which of the music should i start with? maybe the balcony scene in act 1 or the romeo's variation? can you please tell me what i might learn to play to do better?

> Oh it doesn't get better than this.

Juli

Saturday, Apr 19, 8:12 PM

Oh my god Ramon, Ramon I am so so sorry! I practiced my butt off for that audition so I could be close to you!!! You never told me you played viola. I just thought the viola case in your apartment was just where you kept your weed. I can't believe you won the viola audition. I am so depressed. I was gunning through all that traffic to get to the concert and I go to sit down in my new chair and I was looking for you. I had no idea!!! Then I look over during the rests in Juliet's Variation and there you are – on the other side of the pit!!!! I lost it. Mollie looked back at me like WTF and… wait, hold on, entrance coming up…

> That didn't go well. This high stuff is pretty much the reason I gave up the violin in the first place. And now there's Michel giving me his pouty look. GR8. Like everybody doesn't text during the rests. I am just so bummed, Bebe. I can't stand the second violins. Vera's such an airhead. Ramon, this gig just isn't doing it for me, I can't take it. I'm sorry I can't talk to you right now. Crap, gotta play here…

Saturday 9:41 PM

> So I'm turning my ringer back on. I think it's got the Baha Men ring tone. I asked my therapist to call me at 9. In the middle of the quiet part in Act IV. Yup is pretty strict about the no phone rule. He's gonna go ape.
>
> And by the time you turn on your phone back on and get this, it'll all be over for me. I love you and your little fuzzy growths and it's all for the best.

Group MMS

Text Message

Saturday, Apr 19, 11:45 PM

Benni

> Why did she do it? Lee???

Lee

> I do not know why Juli left her ringer on.
> Or why she chose Who Let the Dogs Out.
> All I know is that Romeo kind of freaked out on the stage and lost his grip.
> I'm surprised Juliet survived getting dropped like that.
> It's certainly easy to break a leg on that hard stage floor.
> But when she rolled out over the edge of the stage and into the pit, I knew the viola section was in trouble.
> Now Ramon Gutierrez is day-to-day at Slope Community.
> But Benni, the important thing is we have a teachable moment here.
> A chance to put our differences aside and learn to see beyond the pathetic chunks of strings and wood in our hands.
> And acknowledge that violinists and violists can learn to live together in peace.
> And maybe spend a little less time texting.
> For never was a story more about a phone
> Than this of Juli and her Ramon.

THE ROCKY MOUNTAIN COCHLEA

News and Reviews of Music in Slope County

Cornelius Reichmann

Hard Copy

c. 2008

For 11 years, a local music critic self-published an online journal called The Rocky Mountain Cochlea. Printouts from this publication were discovered among Michel Butrie's personal belongings. Written around the time of his hire, you can see this elderly journalist was very impressed with the young maestro, at least until he wasn't.

The strong opinions of this reviewer appear to have elicited mixed reviews from his readership in various comments sections, though the relationship between a single, eerily supportive reader named Neil Mann and Cornelius Reichmann may never be fully examined.

New Conductor Pays Tribute to Eastern Slope Atrocity: Virtuosic Artistry Inspires!

July 4, 10:53 pm

The atmosphere always feels festive when the Stonehaven Symphony presents its annual free outdoor concert in Central Park. Families arranging their picnic blankets in front of the old bandstand. The sights and sounds of youngsters at play intermingle with those of nearby wildlife. As the tableau of musicians adjusting their wire stands and fastening their scores is silhouetted against dusky funnel clouds on the eastern horizon, we are reminded that long-awaited summer has finally come to the Rocky Mountains.

Before I go any further, I hasten to point out to all of you who read this that I am still taking a hiatus from reviewing. There had been many reasons for this: my lecture and performing engagements as an Honorary Member of the Hans Erich Pfitzner Institut, work around the house, organizing a database for my award-winning Bavarian beer stein collection, and perhaps a touch of mid-life ennui.

Those of you who left comments linking my critique of the Slope Children's Chorale event to the spate of juvenile suicides last month may question the timing of my return or the decision itself, some even asking why. But the reason I have been inspired to take a break from my hiatus is the welcome arrival of Maestro Michel Butrie, A.B.D., the Symphony's new music director. With his searching brown eyes, noble cheekbones, and generous auburn locks, this young maestro's slender build belies, from the audience's dorsal perspective, a sculpted posterior unusual in one so cultivated. That this *wunderkind* has already wrapped his expressive fingers around the very pulse of local *zeitgeist* was evident from the moment he mounted the podium. There he welcomed the modest crowd, acknowledging that "the entire county is suffering in the aftermath of the horrific 'Badminton Massacre'" attack at a local rec center in Eastern Slope. He and the musicians dedicated the concert "not just to the memory of the victims," but also to "the idea that we are all part of a shared humanity." In place of the scheduled opening work, a Rossini trifle, Mr. Butrie proceeded to lead the orchestra in a stirring rendition of the *Merry Widow Overture*. I felt consoled to be amid tens of dozens of true music lovers listening to a beloved work by the Austro-Hungarian master Franz Lehár, a man who knew first-hand the horrors of war, Lehár himself a closet Nazi.

Simply put, Maestro Butrie's interpretation was *wunderbar*. Just the outline of his broad shoulders rippling beneath his tuxedo, the tails of which swung and swayed around his muscled *hintern*, baton thrusting passionately deeper and deeper into the composer's every downbeat, it was a revelation. I sprang up from the crowd brushing grass and alpine guano off my trousers. Then and there I resolved to take the hiatus from my hiatus and personally interview the man at once.

How many times before has this writer seen a disregard of serious music as an Art on the podium, with yet another attempt to make Art "fun." It amazes me that so many impugn the Art that has borne their professional lives from its very loins. While it is Art that makes it possible for us to dream, music is also a basic need of human survival. Music is the language we choose when we are speechless. Not that Michel or I spoke of any of this during the course of our brief, feverish backstage *sitzung*.

I found him reclining between two propane barrels behind the double bass section management had arranged as a make-shift green room. He was pouring over a score covered with little pink Post-It rehearsal notes. I breathlessly introduced myself as writer and editor-in-chief of *The Rocky Mountain Cochlea*. Perhaps he had heard of me? He smiled his boyish smile and cleared his throat before asking me to confirm the spelling.

"Ah, coch-le-a," he said. "Isn't that a part of the human ear?"

"Yes," I replied. Waiting to gauge his intentions, I added, "the inner part."

"Deep. Dark. Hairy," he confirmed, his delicate tenor perhaps trembling somewhat.

Trying to regain my composure I painstakingly explained, "The walls of the hollow cochlea are made of, er, bone, with a thin, delicate lining of epithelial tissue. This is a coiled tube, divided through most of its length by an inner membranous partition. At the top of the snail-shell-like coiling tubes, there is a reversal of the direction of the, er, fluid, thus changing the vestibular duct to the tympanic duct. This continuation at the helicotrema allows fluid being, well, pushed into the vestibular duct by the oval window to move back out via movement in the tympanic duct and deflection of the round window; since the fluid is nearly incompressible and the bony walls are rigid… ah, *Scheisse!*" I cried, clasping him to my bosom.

The relationship between Critic and the Conductor is indeed complex at best. The conductor needs the critic to nourish their ego, for guidance, and when appropriate, for discipline. And in a way, the critic needs the conductor, much as a painter needs a canvas, as an object of fascination on which to lavish his epiphanal emissions. Now, some may pretend they have no use for critics, but critics can make or break a musician's career so it behooves musicians to be friendly. Without being more explicit, I can assure you that some can be very friendly.

After intermission, Mr. Butrie led a simply delightful account of Richard Strauss's *Death and Transfiguration*, a symphonic tone poem of sorts. During one particularly poignant passage, a solo violin line was played with a noble, piercing tone that penetrated even the intermittently-functional microphone dangling in front of the first violins, ably dispatched by Suk-Ling Yu, the orchestra's latest Asian concertmaster.

I must say that in spite of Maestro Butrie's musicianship and the pluck of Ms. Yu, there were at least two young women in the front stands of the orchestra who seemed, to me at least, to be making excessive theatrical movements. Please do not misunderstand me: I am perfectly aware that it takes great energy to be sincere in the aural reproduction of a printed page of music. In addition, there is much emotion involved, as there should be. But the movements became extreme, and it often seemed as if two of the musicians were trying to convince the conductor that they, too, were "feeling" the music. I feel that it is necessary to make a comparison. When one hears the great Berliner Philharmoniker performs, one hears the music. Certainly, the musicians in that organization move as they perform, but it is clear that the music is the first priority. There are no distractions such as tossing of the hair, gazing at the podium in rapture or feigned puppy dog eyes, or females leaning so far forward for a simple page turn that their low-cut *spaltung* spill out in the very face of the music director.

The theme of death and racquet sports was also explored with profound artistry in two additional works. According to the skimpy program notes provided, Debussy's *Jeux* was the composer's homage to three young people searching for a lost tennis ball. The concert ended with a lithe, shapely transcription of Berlioz's *Grand Funereal and Triumphal Symphony*.

To you readers who have never attended the Stonehaven Symphony, I promise you that my use of the word *artistry* was not flippant or used in exaggeration. To those of you who have attended at least *one* of their performances, you know that I do not aggrandize the standing of this organization to any appreciable degree. To those who have already sat through many a season, my point is that Maestro Michel Butrie, A.B.D., is the real thing.

Likewise, my titular use of the word, *atrocity*, in the context of the infamous "Bach, Beethoven, and Badminton" debacle is no exaggeration either. Of course, the pastime was new to Stonehaven in the early

1800s. But that a mistranslation of the word "birdie" in a crate load of imported Badminton instructional sets could have resulted in the indiscriminate bludgeoning of our native turkey vultures is inexcusable. That this outdoor Symphony fundraiser would have had so many "feathered projectiles" circling overhead in the first place, inexplicable.

Following tradition, there were fireworks after the concert. The upstage double bass section emerged unscathed because this year they distanced themselves from the propane tanks behind bandstand with the rest of the ensemble, indeed before the final chord had even died. As the young maestro stepped to either side of musical artists vacating as fast as their legs could carry them, he proclaimed that "these free concerts, which the musicians will not be paid for in any way, shape or form, embody the spirit of this orchestra more than anything else we do."

Posted by Cornelius Reichmann at 10:49 PM

A version of this review appears in print on page C3 of the *Eastern Slope Pioneer Gazette* edition with the headline, "Summer Pleasure, With a Nod to Tragedy."

COMMENTS

5 Comments so far
Leave a comment:

Six middle school suicides in as many weeks – how can you live with yourself, Reichmann? *Comment by Glenn Humpert, July 4 @10:56 pm*

Reichmann, thanks to you my 12-year old is still in counseling. *Comment by Chip Reynolds, July 4 @11:26 pm*

A tragedy, yes. But the Chorale sound is a bit lighter and more balanced now. *Comment by Cornelius Reichmann, July 4 @11:06 pm*

Shame! *Comment by Marilyn Smithson July 4 @ 10:26 pm*

So many of us have missed you and your unflinching acumen, Mr. Reichmann! *Comment by Neil Mann, July 5 @ 1:29 am*

Excellence Attained: The Artistic Virtuosity of Hans Erich Pfitzner

March 1 10:18 pm

As I have said before, we live in a culture that puts music in the arts and entertainment section of newspapers, but art has never had anything to do with entertainment. Unsung 20th century German musical heroes such as composer Hans Erich Pfitzner instinctively knew this. I myself have been a concert pianist for 72 years (as well as an Honorary Member of the Hans Erich Pfitzner Institut and an award-winning Bavarian beer stein collector). I never had the self-image of being an entertainer, nor did I ever feel that I had to sell anything at any performance. If only Symphony Board President Glenn Humpert and the rest of the board possessed a fraction of this integrity.

But imagine my delight upon discovering that director Michel Butrie, A.B.D., had succeeded in persuading the Board to program a themed concert including two works by Hans Erich Pfitzner himself. Yes, it required some behind-the-scenes "lobbying" with the maestro. It required a few symphony board member resignations. Wine was poured, money changed hands, sheets were soiled, but wisdom prevailed, and last Saturday evening the Stonehaven Symphony subscribers finally were able to experience *Music Approved of by the Third Reich*.

The concert began with Beatrice Sara, the Symphony's homely Principal Oboist, who went from zero to hero as soloist in Johann Nepomuk Hummel's *Introduction, Theme, and Variations*, Op. 102. Hummel succeeded Haydn at the court of Prince Esterházy and composed the work not long after he was dismissed for inattention to duties in 1824. His *hausmusik* house concert arrangements also appealed to the Third Reich, which viewed them as an opportunity for communal control a century later. Ms. Sara's glacial performance belied Mr. Butrie's command of the long thin white stick Almighty *Gott* graced him with and with which he brought out the autumnal beauties of this masterpiece.

The concert proceeded with Mozart's final *Symphony No. 41*. Mr. Humpert's vestigial program notes made mention of the fact that Mozart was declared the greatest German genius by Hitler's Propaganda Minister, Joseph Goebbels, but erred with the claim that Mozart soon after died of a heart attack, which he did not. He died of an anaerobic infection similar to gangrene. This fact has been known for 12 years or more. We know this because individuals, including his oldest son, have commented on how the room was so full of the foul odor of the infection and Mozart's body so swollen that no one except his wife Constanze could even approach his deathbed.

By the *Symphony*'s final chord, the sickly sweet aroma of the Symphony Guild ladies' cookies and crepes had filled the auditorium, and blessed intermission had arrived.

After intermission came the highpoint: a rare North American performance of not one but two works by Hans Erich Pfitzner. Hans Erich Pfitzner was born in Moscow in 1869. The central event of Pfitzner's life was the annexation of Strasbourg by France in the aftermath of World War I, when he lost his livelihood, left destitute at age 50. When the Nazis came to power in 1933, he was recruited to lecture for the Militant League for German Culture. By 1945, his home had been destroyed in the war by Allied bombing, and the composer found himself an aging, half-insane street person.

Before I go any further with this critique, I must emphasize that I would never desire to denigrate Maestro Butrie, a truly butyraceous conductor and human being who against all odds successfully campaigned to program *Music Approved of by the Third Reich* in the first place. The only challenge the musicians faced for this program was simply executing Pfitzner's printed notes.

For the rest of the English-speaking world, Pfitzner's only challenge simply lies in the correct pronunciation of his name: you must firmly grip your lower lip between your teeth and exhale violently before taking your tongue and buckling it against the roof of your mouth. Try it. You're probably closer to the correct sound than, say, the Stonehaven Symphony during its assault of the *Small Symphony in G major* last night. As I had tried to explain to the young maestro before the first rehearsal, you can lead a soldier to water, but sometimes he's just going to drown.

"Are you certain the orchestra will be up to the challenge?" I called up to him on the empty stage.

"They're not going to like this music," Michel moaned.

"Yes, well, I've seen them on this stage for years," I said, pacing back and forth below the podium. "They look miserable. Do they like anything?"

"They're musicians. They like it when they get paid." He thoughtfully licked a frothy head of *Hefeweisen* from his upper lip and slid the mug back to me. "Getting out of rehearsal early. And short rehearsals. Yes, I would say getting out of rehearsal early and short rehearsals." He freed a lusty belch.

"Yes, well, now they're going to have to learn to like probing journalism."

"Cornelius," he pleaded, leaping up from his fetal position. "I don't know what the board's going to do to me if the orchestra gets another review like your last one."

"Take Humpert's mind off how bad the orchestra sounds. Just do what everybody else does and fire the concertmaster."

"But I like Suk-Ling," he said. "She laughs at my jokes."

"*Scheisse*, man," I cried. "She doesn't even have a green card. When she tries to read the sticky notes you give her, her lips move. She doesn't understand a damn thing you said!"

A look of wonder crossed his face. "She does laugh a lot."

But after tonight's debacle, I am left at a loss for diplomatic critique, at a loss for words. I will never be able to wipe away the memory of the inexorable slump of Maestro Butrie's once erect backbone as the lower strings, with their clouded intonation and buzzy, rattling tone, fairly laid waste to Pfitzner's *Cracow Greetings,* Though I am reminded of the year 1939 and that Polish city mayor's plea, *"Feuer einstellen! Feuer einstellen!",* as German *Luftwaffe* descended upon his defenseless population.

Posted by Cornelius Reichmann at 10:18 PM

A version of this review appears in print on page C3 of the *Eastern Slope Pioneer Gazette* edition with the headline, "Don't Give Hate a Baton."

COMMENTS

3 Comments so far
Leave a comment:

This music no good. I feel dirty. *Comment by Suk-Ling Yu, March 1 @ 11:26 pm*

The childrens' memorial services were quite beautiful, Reichmann. Your name was mentioned several times. "Cornelius Reichmannus." It really has a ring to it in when a priest says it in the Latin, don't you think? *Comment by Glenn Humpert, March 1 @11:56 pm*

My little son now just lies in bed staring up at the ceiling all day, playing with his feeding tubes. Your newspaper review of his Children's Chorale solo is crumpled in his little clenched fist. My wife says if I was a man, I would seek vengeance for what you have done. *Comment by Chip Reynolds, March 2 @ 12:22 am*

If you were a man, you would have been out playing ball with your son instead of enrolling him in a choir. Lighten up! *Comment by Cornelius Reichmann, March 2 @ 12:26 am*

Another Stonehaven Symphony Finale: I Am Taking a Hiatus

May 16 10:58 pm

Beethoven's *Ninth Symphony* is quite a crowd-pleasing work to have in an orchestra's back pocket and work up at a moment's notice. The fact that Maestro Michel Butrie had also programmed the immortal *meisterstück* for orchestra and chorale only a few months back didn't detract from last Saturday's performance in the slightest. After all, there are only a couple dozen warhorses that will pry the typical Classical concert-goer out of their rockers to purchase tickets, and the *Ninth* would be right there at the top. This was the Stonehaven Symphony's final concert of the season. It was also possibly the last concert before the forced retirements of some of the older, more wizened, faces in the ensemble. Many of these individuals have cakes of bow rosin older than Maestro Butrie. Ironically, as the great circle of life in the symphony turns to its grisly conclusion and if the Board has its way, this sad pageant may well include the maestro himself.

Mr. Butrie was in fact compelled to program something more familiar due to the public outcry following the previous concert (see "Third Reich," above). Many were unable to comprehend the fact that true Art does not know fads or political correctness. It is Art that makes it possible for us to dream. As I've said many times, music is a basic need of human survival. Music is the language we choose when we are speechless.

Come to find out, some of the actual musicians were not speechless after all (see "I feel dirty"). Not to be outdone, some subscribers could be seen protesting on the sidewalk in front of the auditorium, brandishing various inflammatory posters, including "Don't Give Hate a Baton" and "Snuff-haven Symphony." To be fair, there was also a lively counter-protest, including well-shaven men with confederate flags and "Gentile Lives Matter" placards as well as others I could not make out in the flickering light of automobiles still burning in the parking lot at press time.

Michel was beside himself. Knowing as this writer did that our vision had not been well-received and that the orchestra board wanted the maestro's auburn-locked head on a spit, this writer sought him out in the green room before the concert, but he was inconsolable.

"But what did the board think about this glowing review?" I exclaimed, pushing my reading glasses back onto my nose and scrolling though my laptop for the latest Rocky Mountain Cochlea.

"Glenn says it's anti-Semitic," he said.

"Anti-Semitic my *arsch*," I cried, "Humpert wouldn't know a Semite if it shook his uncircumsized…"

"I just want to be taken seriously!" he pounded his delicate fists on the divan. "The players all make jokes about me. Suk-Ling stopped laughing after the last concert set. Now, every time I stop the cellos and change her bowings, I'll see her slip her phone out and start thumbing through TripAdvisor. Somebody's putting inappropriate pink sticky notes in my score. That big German bass soloist you wanted, von Tramp or whatever his name is—he says he wants to 'make me his *hund*.' Whatever that means. Cornelius, what does that even mean?"

I tried to console the boy, trying to hold his head down in my lap and stroking his tawny hair like we used to, but he would have none of it. He proceeded to call this writer some hurtful names that I'm sure he would have taken back had he not also been somewhat winded from swinging his old Hans Erich Pfitzner *Cracow Greetings* score at me. For that moment before impact, I stood there and marveled at the sheer passion of this young Adonis, his puppy dog eyes bulging, biceps flaring, moisture gathering in his underarm area. Clearly, he requires the guidance of a more mature mentor, a passionate mentor like myself who could reap the fruits of his youth. But as the thick score fairly disintegrated against my temple and I lost consciousness, I remembered that it is Art which makes it possible for us to dream.

Indeed, I remember dreaming I was floating down a river, birds singing, the fruity aroma of Bavarian field hops in the air, not a care in the world. Perched on the hills above me, fantastic medieval castles echoing with the fables and songs of bygone Nibelungs. It was idyllic, and I might have felt more tranquil and at peace than I have in years had it not been for a mysterious rhythmic tugging from beneath my swim trunks.

However, as a result of being thusly incapacitated, I was unable to evaluate the first work on the program, Erwin Schulhoff's 1921 *Suite for Chamber Orchestra*, Op. 37. It was no doubt an olive branch extended to the Board as it did feature that individual who happened to reside for a time at the Wülzburg concentration death camp facility. In general, though, Schulhoff's music suffers from the malaise of so many modern composers, and I don't refer here to the tuberculosis from which he succumbed but the equally morbid compulsion to explore new musical ideas regardless of merit. What are these so-called "modern" composers trying to prove? Certainly, the better approach would have been to go with just the Beethoven and let it stand alone as one of the most remarkable pieces of music of all time. I have no regrets about missing the Schulhoff piece whatsoever.

Due to the nature of a gaping head wound, I was indisposed for most of the Beethoven itself. However, I do think that after having covered the Stonehaven Symphony for 72 years, I have a pretty good idea of what it sounded like. No doubt, there was a little fuzzy entrance from the woodwinds around measure sixteen, but they quickly recovered and proceeded to the end of the first movement without any miscues. The string entrances under the leadership of Oriental concertmaster Suk-Ling Yu as usual resembled lost orphans in search of a firearm with which to put themselves out of their misery. And not to be picky, but there was a flub in the French horn.

It was only a matter of time before I came to out in the lobby where the young maestro had deposited my body next to a group of long-time Symphony donors from the local hospice. Slapping away the hands of one senile fugitive who had attempted to affix her catheter to my privates, I could hear the musicians launching into the final movement in the distance. Their excitement was palpable, their concentration, acute, their intonation, suspect. They were bringing that special energy to the final movement that comes from the players' sense of actual discovery and that special thrill born of the fear that it might all go horribly wrong.

The final movement brings all the previous movements themes back to stormy exhilaration with a frenetic entrance that stops abruptly and shifts focus to the ensemble of sonorous double basses. Beethoven loved his double basses, and he did good by them here by having them introduce one of the most evocative melodies in Western music. They, in turn, ecstatically accepted the challenge, almost as if still giddy from their brush with death at the July 4th concert (see "Eastern Slope Atrocity"). As the theme repeats it is taken over by different instruments and then by just about everyone on stage before things take a turn for the dramatic as it is handed off to the Bass Vocal Soloist.

Well, stop the presses: this healthy fellow is the real thing. One big *bruder*, with considerable enunciation and articulation in his sovereign instrument that established beyond the shadow of a doubt this man was an actual pure-bred *Deutscher*. I feverishly pressed what was left of my reading glasses to my face, searching Humpert's unintelligible program notes for his name. Von Trapp? Van Trammel? Whoever he was, he appeared to be a native of the Munich region of Bavaria and not so far from the delightful stretch of the Rhine river where I spent many of my own formative years. I cast down the program and feasted my eyes on this German steed, his mane of blond hair wisped around his prominent forehead like a halo. The words he sang, taken from Friedrich von Schiller and adapted by Beethoven, "All men become brothers, where your tender wing lingers, be embraced, millions, this kiss to the entire world, brothers, above starry canopy," they struck at my prostate like a thunderbolt.

There on the stage, this hulking specimen loomed over the young maestro, a man over a boy, like a barnyard stallion over a goat. To either side, what was left of the Slope Children's Chorale rose as one, pubescent girls and boys in their matching uniforms and larger boys, boys whose voices had chosen that very moment, those very notes, to crack into manhood, the entire menagerie coming to life with a whole new level of primordial dissonance.

The other soloists stood for their turns. The tenor, at least, demonstrated the kind of opulent voice I think works best for this piece, as opposed to the reedy timbre heard so many regional performances. Having a tenor with some *cojones* helped to make the soprano and mezzo-soprano stand out in contrast, more matronly, not that these local veterans needed much help in that department as far as I could see. It was a bit hard to see from my discrete vantage, concealed off to the side of the rear handicap ramp as I was, due to the fact the maestro had deposited me in the lobby without my trousers.

Indeed, after much consideration, I have decided to revisit my hiatus. I began this blog site in 1997, but I wrote and published reviews for three years before that. Since that time, I have written over 1200 reviews, and I now wish to direct my efforts to other projects. I would like to express my gratitude for all you readers for enjoying *The Rocky Mountain Cochlea* and commenting on the various articles as so many of you saw fit to do. I know that many times my views have disturbed some of you who spent the time reading my articles. I make no apology for that because my conviction of the importance of music *as an Art* was instilled in me by my very first piano teacher 72 years ago. For me, music has never been a "pastime" or something that I did for "fun."

I look forward to some quiet time, perhaps abroad, in a more secluded area of Bavaria, where I might enlarge my award-winning stein collection. Lest any *Cochlea* haters out there should become over-zealous, you should be aware Germany now employs a substantial neighborhood watch, citizen police, with pepper spray. Who knows, with the aid of their robust witness protection program that has enabled so many in my profession to go on to lead normal lives, perhaps true love may yet wait for me upon the banks of the Rhine not so far from Munich. I will keep this site active because I fully intend to write occasional articles when inspiration strikes, when I feel something in the world of music needs comment, or whenever my ego feels like it. For music is the language we choose, but only when we are actually speechless.

As for the concert, the Slope Children's Chorale rose one last time for the climactic final cadences, their unspeakable harmonies merging with the instruments themselves, ultimately bringing down the house with a spectacular finish. Members of the audience who were still responsive after the 90-minute spectacle erupted for a sustained 15 solid seconds of deafening and hand-numbing applause. Perhaps not so long by Berliner Philharmoniker standards though ample time to scare the *scheisse* out of any who hoped they had fallen asleep.

Posted by Cornelius Reichmann at 11:49 PM

A version of this review appears in print on page C1 of the *Eastern Slope Pioneer Gazette* edition with the headline, "Reichmann Surrenders."

COMMENTS

3 comments so far
Leave a comment:
Shame!!!! *Comment by Marilyn Smithson, May 17 @11:59 pm*

Sieg Heil! Mr. Reichmann, you shall be missed and revered forever. *Comment by Neil Mann, May 18 @12:00 am*

I will find you. *Comment by Chip Reynolds, May 18 @ 12:29 am*

CURIOUS GEORGE AND HIS LITTLE BROWN BUGLE

Michel Butrie, DMA, and Staff

Google Doc

2012

The Mountain Vista Women's Correctional Facility was home to a population that showed absolutely no concern for human life. The opportunity to perform there was evidently too good to pass up for Stonehaven Symphony administrators, but it did present some challenges. Here we can actually see how Michel Butrie and the musicians edited their usual Family Fun Extravaganza program just in time for a Mountain Vista Women's Correctional Facility debut!

Curious George and His Little Brown Bugle

Stonehaven Symphony Orchestra
~~Family Fun Extravaganza~~
<u>Mountain Vista Women's Correctional Facility</u>
Concert Script
Conceived, written, and created by Maestro Michel Butrie, DMA

<u>Final Draft</u>

> michel your kids program is great you've been tweaking it but please we need something anything different for womens prison concert today (Yup Michaels) Today, 06:48 am

MB: Good afternoon and welcome to this very special *Behind The Symphony*™ educational performance entitled Curious George and His Little Brown Bugle. My name is Maestro Michel Butrie and together we are going to explore some of the most inspirational music ever written.

MB conducts *Pavane pour une infante défunte*

(Applause here) MB: That was a song by Maurice Ravel called Pavane for a Dead Princess. Didn't it sound like music for a princess? Did it make you feel like a princess, too? Just a little? Who here is excited? I'm excited. Let's begin.

I'm sure you all remember the story of Curious George, "a curious little brown monkey who was captured in Africa by The Man in the Yellow Hat." (Put on hat.) That's me! (Laughter here) Now where is that little brown monkey? Where did he go? Are there any little brown monkeys out there? Well, I'll give you a hint: in the story about Curious George's trip to the dinosaur museum, the animal show director says "I have a bugle for you right here." Well, what better place to find a bugle than a symphony orchestra! Who knows what a symphony orchestra is? Oh, look at all that waving! Let's see, how about... (Here I choose a ~~smaller child~~ <u>less violent predator</u> in front who cannot be clearly heard by others.) ...you!

> note there may be african-american individuals present (Parker DeVon) Yesterday, 02:45 pm

> parker you are so full of it there are no black people in stonehaven (Vera Azaduzi) Yesterday, 02:47 pm

> but they may still be in the penal system (Parker DeVon) Yesterday, 02:56 pm

"A skilled ensemble of classical musicians who must follow the conductor's baton"? ~~Bravo!~~ <u>Tight!</u> Well, now you can pretend you're a big conductor like me and move your ~~fingers~~ <u>handcuffs</u> around in the air while we listen to the beautiful *Morgenstemning*, music composer Edvard Grieg wrote for a scene in a play. This music depicts a man in a tree beating apes off with a stick.

MB conducts "Morning Mood"

(Applause) MB: Speaking of excited apes: look at all that musical talent out there! And look, here comes our little brown monkey! (Principal Trumpet Pedro Martinez enters dressed in Curious George's green coat and cap.)

> note an individual of latino descent may not be appropriate for this role (Parker DeVon) Yesterday, 03:01 pm

Remember in the story, where Curious George tries to feed his little bugle to a big tall ostrich bird? Well, he's walking right over to our Principal Bassoon player Abigail Peck. It looks like Pedro's going to try to ram his bugle right down her big tall bassoon! ~~Silly monkey!~~ That ape's buck wild! Let's hear what her bassoon solo sounds like now in Gaetano Donizetti's *L'Elisir d'amour*:

> dont think pedro is hispanic but sunburns easily (Yup Michaels) Yesterday, 04:25 pm

> even so offenders should see diverse individuals of color on stage (Yup Michaels) Yesterday, 04:26 pm

MB conducts "The Elixir of Love"

(Applause) MB: Thank you so much! And remember what happened at the end of the story, when Curious George walked into the dinosaur museum? "George saw something so enormous, it took his breath away. It was a dinosaur." (Here Pedro walks behind Principal Double Bass Ludmilla Popov, climbs onto her stool and grasps her scroll with both hands.)

> note plenty of diversity women in orchestra making a difference 86% are women not counting harleen (Parker DeVon) Yesterday, 11:30 pm

"He climbed up the dinosaur's neck and started to pull. Crash." (Here I arrive and playfully push Pedro off Belinda's stool.) "Guards came rushing in from all sides, and underneath the fallen dinosaur, they found a little monkey."

> note brochure says women at mountain vista maximum security location "show absolutely no concern for human life" (Lee Chuk) Yesterday, 11:35 pm

What do you think they said to that little brown monkey? I bet those guards ~~were pretty disappointed~~ ripped George a new one.

What fun we've had here at beautiful ~~Cherry Hill Family Fun Center~~ Mountain Vista Women's Correctional. Don't these inspirational, life-changing classical masterworks make you want to ~~learn a musical instrument of your own~~ get up and shake your booties? (Cheers) Now I'm really excited! Let's conclude our Curious George and the Stonehaven Symphony program with a special performance of Francis Poulenc's *Les mamelles de Tirésias* just for all you ~~talented kids~~ phat homegirls!

> awesome listen i am tired of doing crap gigs like now this orchestra pimping around for funding buckage (Crowley Davids) Yesterday, 11:39 pm

> and here we will be killed (Vera Azaduzi) Yesterday, 02:53pm

Come visit us again soon... *Behind The Symphony*™!

> soon but after your remaining jail time has been served (Yup Michaels) Yesterday, 04:38 pm

MB conducts "The Breasts of Tiresias"

(Applause)

STICKY NOTES

Michel Butrie, DMA, and Unknown Contributor

Pencil on Paper Sticky Notes

2009

Orchestra directors like Maestro Michel Butrie worked with large musical scores and had to jot down quick musician cues, corrections, and reminders for themselves while they were conducting rehearsals. Often the quickest way to do this was with yellow Post-its or "sticky notes." But when a veritable treasure trove of these little artifacts was discovered at the archaeological site, researchers made an amazing discovery: there, nestled between the Maestro's entries, was the handwriting of a second author!

What would you do if somebody else was writing on your sticky notes?

> 3/25 Tchaikovsky Rehearsal
>
> Bring briefcase, baton, scores, banana
>
> Keep hydrated
>
> Remember: don't slouch, look intense, check fly

> **WHEN PEOPLE GET TO KNOW ME THEY REALLY LIKE ME.**
>
> Get clock from Yup
>
> Find out who's leaving inappropriate sticky notes in score.
>
> Careful with podium (big step up) this time
>
> Tell orchestra they did good job last weekend.
>
> String spots much improved
>
> Horn articulations did not sound "flatulent" (Reichmann's concert review way off base)
>
> (NOTE: Mutes for next weekend)

EVERYDAY, IN EVERY WAY,
I AM GETTING BETTER AND BETTER

Don't forget to tune
(short black thing in back/right = oboe)

Start Rehearsal Strong

Say SOMETHING INSPIRATIONAL

What Tchaikovsky called the 5th Symphony:

"a complete resignation before fate"

CORRECTION:
Wikipedia says "Allegro con anima"
does too mean
"Quick with animation"
(not "Quick rectal cleanse")

Start at M. 38 – Cue clarinet
(other short black thing in back)

But don't make him nervous with
eye contact

S-l-o-w upbeat, do not freak him
out

Do not forget what he did
to the Brahms last concert

I FORGIVE ANYONE WHO
HAS HURT ME IN THE PAST.

ITS ME AGAIN !

XOXO

Mvt II "Animando"

(Italian: look up in Wikipedia – "like animals"?)

Measure 144 – String duplets –> <u>What</u> <u>The</u> <u>Heck</u>?

Nobody is counting. Everybody is lost.

DEPRESSION IS JUST A STEPPING STONE

Tell them practice <u>on</u> <u>your</u> <u>own</u> at home.

8:30 PM – Break Time
(They hate when you forget!)

Leave podium quickly (don't trip), go to dressing room

Do not make eye contact with Pedro the Trumpet Player (dent was probably already there)

or creepy Principal Second Violin with the piercings

8:45 PM – Mvt III "Valse"

Fix Cellos (too slow/heavy)

Horns and brass are Way Too Slow!

"Valse" Is A Dance
("Valise" is a baggage)

What's Creepy Girl's name?
She's always staring at me.

Mollie?

Make her stop writing down
everything you say

Just Play!!

Measure 89 — Second Violins -> What The Heck?

Try to sing the phrasing for the violins again.

(I think they like it)

Can't Molly cue them with her bow? Does she ever blink?

Ask new concertmaster ("Peng-Peng"? Sp.?) for bowing advice

Tell them This Is Unacceptable! with a big strong voice.

Make each violin stand/play part alone. Set the tone!

I EXUDE PURPOSE AND JOY

FORGIVE ME IF THIS IS COMPLETLY INAPROPRIATE. I DON'T KNOW HOW ELSE TO SAY IT WITHOUT GETTING TACKY.

EVERY MORNING I WATCH YOUR APARTMENT WINDOW

JUST TO SEE YOUR SHADOWS ON THE CURTAIN.

I WANT U 2 B MY BABY DADDY!!

Mvt IV "Finale"

Not working out. Definitely mute horns

Measure 1: Stringed instruments already out-of-tune

CORRECTION: there is too a low F double-sharp on the violin:

Tell them it's supposed to be just the G-string with no fingers.

Measure 392 — it's only poco crescendo

(The long brown things in back are too loud too fast)

Vln II (esp. Mollie) –

Don't stop playing and write down every single thing I say. Don't pull out the nose ring during the rests, don't jab it back in and smile at me like that

Just Play!!!!

Q for Yup: Can we please fire Mollie for something?

I KNOW YOUR SCEDULE.

YOU DO HAVE TIME FOR ME

Measure 418 — now brown things can be loud

Then at Measure 428 – "Sempre con tutta forza"

(Tell them this means "very loud")

Too wimpy! Keep playing loud!

Measure 436 — It's supposed to be "Molto Vivace" – much faster!

They're not even paying attention, they're just smiling at each other.
Tell them: Watch my beat!!

I LOVE AND RESPECT MY BODY

NOTE: Move arms faster.

ALL THE BANANAS IN YOUR BRIEFCASE TASTE CONFUSING. U SHOULD EAT ORANGES WHICH HAVE VITAMINS FOR YOUR MUSCLES.

Measure 482 — Everybody needs to be even louder than before.

It's just all too weak. Like diarrhea. Figure out something to tell them.

Horns should blow harder

Why do flutes always sound so soft and depressing?

STRING PLAYERS RESPECT CONDUCTORS

WHO MAKE EDUCATED SUGGESTIONS

BUT QUICKLY BECOME SUSPICIOUS.

Q for concertmaster: can violins maybe put on louder strings?

IS MY PERSONALITY CAPTIVATING AND INTERESTING?

> I SEE YOU LOOKING AT THAT NEW CONCERTMASTER!
>
> PENGPENG DOES EVERYTHING YOU SAY.
>
> BUT SHE'LL NEVER LOVE YOU LIKE ME!!
>
> WHY CAN'T YOU SEE!!!

> Measure 490 — fff — as loud as you can play
>
> Trumpets "marciale, energico" = "like energetic soldiers"
>
> Strings JUST ALL TOO WIMPY
>
> Ask new concertmaster can they press down the bows harder?
>
> (And Where is Peng-Peng? Why doesn't she come anymore?)

> I LUV MY LOUD CONDUCTOR BOI SOOOO MUCH!!!
>
> U MAKE ME THINK EVIL THOUHTS.
>
> I WANNA SURPRISE YOU W/SOMETHING SPECIAL

> Measure 503 – sfff – Everybody in the back should be blowing their long black/brown things as hard as they can
>
> Measure 504 – Presto – even faster
>
> And let Lee know you heard him telling cellos to fake it!
>
> Maybe Peng-Peng has a bowing?
>
> NOTE: Where the heck did Peng-Peng go?
>
> Measure 546 – ffff – More More MORE!
>
> I'M INTERCONNECTED
>
> WITH EVERYTHING IN THE UNIVERSE

End rehearsal on time (10:00 pm?)

(Yup says orchestra players have families)

Ask Yup about where is Peng-Peng

Check where funny smell is coming from.

Leave quickly

(but do not trip)

NOW WE CAN FINALLY BE TOGETHER!!!!

DON'T LOOK UNDER THE PODIUM. (NOISES SHOULD SUBSIDE W/TIME)

THE GINGERBREAD MAN

Personnel Manager Yup Michaels

Hardcopy Printout

2013

Yup Michaels' body was never recovered. But some 25 feet beyond the tour bus front bumper, near a briefcase linked to him, scattered pages were unearthed. Among them, the official record of an internal sexual harassment investigation!

Listen to first a recorded interview with musician Abigail Peck, then jumbled fragments of evidentiary lists, then back to Abigail and garbled snippets of Beatrice Sara, each lovingly transcribed with Yup's own Shorthand for Nonverbal Behavior at the end. See Harleen "Harles" Marie interview too, investigative procedures, and even a holiday cookie recipe, a veritable time capsule of 21st century orchestra life.

Now you too can sort through all the evidence and find the real predator!

YM   Okay, we're recording. It is presently 1835 hours on November 17, 2013. I, Stonehaven Symphony Orchestra Personnel Administrator, Yup Michaels, have been charged with an interview of Abigail Peck of the Bassoon Section, aka "Witness No. 3."

Abby, I want to start off with some basic info down here that we can, um, get ironed out for the report. Your first name is spelled A-B-I-G-A-I-L and Peck is spelled P-E-C-K, correct?

AP   Why are you asking me all this? (breaks down in tears)

YM   Okay. Okay. Now, Abby, you're not the one who's getting investigated here, right? You're one of our witnesses. Maybe I can just, uh, tell you what you told me? And you can just nod your head? If you agree?

AP   (nods)

YM   Okay, your name is Abigail Peck. You've been with the Symphony for six years, right?

AP   (sniffles)

YM   Abby, I know we're going to be talking about some things that are deeply emotional. I'm so sorry to have to ask you to relive that night. But we've got to do due diligence. We just need to ask a few preliminary questions, okay? Okay. So Maestro Michel Butrie promoted you to Principal Bassoon in January of 2007, right? After a formal, competitive audition. Including two rounds?

AP   (nods and sniffles)

YM   Good. Now, everybody followed the rules for your promotion. There was nobody who, um, deviated from official union protocol. For example, you didn't have access to any preparation assistance that other auditioning individuals didn't have access to.

AP   (begins to sob uncontrollably)

YM   And none of the audition committee, nobody communicated confidential information, you wouldn't have gotten inappropriate knowledge of specific repertoire selections, right?

AP   (unintelligible)

YM   Or, um, had sexual relations with any member of the audition committee?

AP   Well, (sniffs), just Pedro. Afterward, by the loading dock. We kinda celebrated.

Summary of key evidence: *List the items collected for the investigation and how or from whom they were obtained.*

Not formally authorized to collect this evidence, as per federal law. This civilian lacked jurisdiction and also aptitude. However, at approximately 2000 on November 15, I was able to investigate the assigned Women's Dressing Room during a dress rehearsal of the Arabian Dance oboe solo the (Alleged) Harasser was playing during Pyotr Ilyich Tchaikovsky's Nutcracker Ballet. Personal effects were located next to the door by the hallway. Though several individuals were visible on the floor area, dressing table was neat and organized. The following items were noted on or by the dressing table next to the door:

Altieri Oboe and Laptop Gig Bag.

iPhone 3G, red case, Winter Wonderland screen saver

(2) hair clips

Jones 101MS oboe reeds – Medium-Soft (3 Pack)

French Style Reed Case

Gem double-ended silk swab

Doctor Slick Cork Grease

Fruit cake (in wrapper, half eaten)

Twizzlers Pull 'N' Peel Cherry Chewy Candy Bag

1) Misc.

Handel *Messiah* sheet music from last week

"My Rod" English horn part from last pops concert, stained (possibly ketchup)

Oboe Woes (a novel)

Desiccated plant material. Oval leaves, waxy, white berries, with attached hook.

(3) Stonehaven High side-by-side student musicians (on floor area, unconscious)

Also, Lancy the librarian (on floor area, also unconscious)

Portable cassette player (Tomashi)

AP   It was hard to see her like that. (sniffle) You could tell she'd been through a lot. There was loss in her eyes. You know, when a woman has been forced against her will to experience something she never asked for? Or deserved? I knew she would never be the same again. At least, I hoped she wouldn't be.

YM   What do you mean? How?

AP   Her voice was all croaky. (Openly weeping and holding out her hand) This fingernail was broken!

YM. Sweet Jesus!

AP   It was crazy. And it had been going on so long. I should have said something. I should have spoken up. But I didn't. I, I chose peace over drama. Does that make me a bad person?

YM   But you stated you weren't even there when it happened, right?

AP   No. No, I must have gotten there right after. I was too late.

YM   But you saw her then? What did she say?

AP   She said... she said she felt dead. She said she couldn't feel anything anymore. I, I tried to put my arm around her, Yup, but she pushed me away! She pushed me... away. She said she didn't want to be touched...

YM   Didn't want to be touched again?

AP   ... then she pushed me against the wall! I still have a bruise on my elbow. You can see it here, and here...

YM   Abby, would you say she was acting differently? Differently than usual?

AP   ... (crying hysterically) She never thought it would happen to her...

YM   Okay. Okay. And did she say anything more? Anything more about what happened to her?

AP   I can't, Yup, it's too real...

YM   I know, I know. But we've got to talk about this. Do you understand? We've got to stop this from ever happening to anyone else ever again!

AP   Yup, she said she had never felt more like, like she wanted to kill somebody, in her life!

YM   Oh, man. And that's saying a lot for Harleen.

- (1) voicemail time stamped Sat Nov 9 21:06:57 from "Ramon Gutierrez" to "Harleen Maris."

- (36) text messages from time stamp Sat Nov 9 21:07:18 from "Harleen Maris" to "Yup Michaels."

- Food Testing. Colorado Department of Public Health & Environment. Analysis report from Dec 2, Bakery Sample No. 206 ("no cannabis or hallucinogens detected").

- (1) audio recording of loud music audible from basement dressing room area during Nutcracker Ballet dress rehearsal on November 16 provided by Mr. Yup Michaels, Personnel Manager.

- Transcript of 911 call during unsanctioned wind section holiday party, August 31.

- Surveillance camera from Slope Auditorium woodwind dressing room recorded on November 15. (footage 19:55:00 – 20:05:00 appears to be missing).

- iPhone video footage of Slope Auditorium loading dock taken from a concealed vantage by Mr. Parker DeVon, Musicians Representative on the Symphony Board, Miscellaneous Advisory Sub-Committee, August 29 (2007).

Findings of Fact

- At 22:39 on January 29, 2007, Pedro Martinez and Abigail Peck approach the Slope Auditorium loading dock area immediately following the woodwind audition held at nearby St. Crispin Church. Ms. Peck is visible crying, possibly tears of joy. Mr. Martinez can be heard congratulating Ms. Peck on her embouchure. She proceeds to place her hand on Mr. Martinez's pelvic area and attempts to embrace him. He then is seen restraining Ms. Peck. They fall over onto a flower bed under the permit parking sign.

  Approximately one minute later, the stage door by the trash compactor above them swings open. A large black garbage bag is being squeezed through the doorway by a shadowy figure. The garbage bag, obscuring an individual's identity, moves toward the camera. Ms. Peck can be seen rolling off Mr. Martinez and tearfully apologizing in the background, but a woman's voice interrupts her, saying, "Can't take it anymore. I just can't take it anymore. If I have to listen to this Christmas crap one more time, I'm gonna gag myself." Opening the bag directly above the camera, what appear to be Nutcracker Ballet orchestral parts tumble out onto the camera obscuring the video. "I won't tell if you don't," the voice continues before there is an audible gasp and Stonehaven Symphony Librarian Lancy Headney can be seen peering directly down into the camera and shrieking, "Oh, my God, Parker? Parker, get out of the dumpster!"

These facts are supported by the iPhone video footage in MOV format and attached hereto as Exhibit B.

I thought she wanted it. That's what she was saying.

YM   Okay. So, first, you are admitting you were, you know, in the room together…

BS   Duh, it's our dressing room, I wanted to fit it before rehearsal! There wasn't much time.

YM   Sure, yes. Was the door closed?

BS   Yeah, we closed the door. Fatima's kind of shy. She's very nervous, but I was, like, "Just relax. We'll have plenty of time over the holidays, too!"

YM   You could see Fatima was nervous?

BS   Nervous, but I think she was excited too. She was torn between the emotions.

YM   She was uncomfortable with the situation. And you could see that.

BS   Yeah. Well, no, auditioning makes everybody uncomfortable. That's why I thought…

YM   Did hear her say "stop?"

BS   Um, what?

YM   Did. You. Hear. Her. Say. Stop?

BS   "Stop?" Well, yes. Sure. They all say, "Stop."

YM   You heard her say "stop." and you kept doing it? Wait, "they?" "They" who? How many have there been?

BS   Well, Yup. You know I get pretty excited this time of year. It's just my little thing. It's not like I'm hurting anybody.

YM   It's not like you're hurting anyone? Listen to me: "Malicious intent is not required for an act to be deemed unwanted."

BS   An act? What act?

YM   No means no!

BS   Yup, this is ridiculous. What's wrong with it? It was just a little fun. We're all musicians, anyway. We all do music, and that's all this is!

YM   I don't know about that, Bea. If threatening victims' dignity and psychological or physical health creating a toxic work or environment is what musicians do, we have harassment.

Witness No. 2 stated that this behavior started out as a "Secret Santa" game where the (Alleged) Harasser smiled creepily and started giving him candy canes when he would go backstage. However, this grooming behavior quickly escalated into a weekly occurrence after every rehearsal. Initially the individual played the music quite softly in the dressing rooms downstairs from a portable cassette player, but over time the music got louder and louder. Eventually, the Witness began to feel "nauseated" and "deafened" when the music started coming on every time he walked into his dressing room are and stated, "That fruit bat just don't know when to stop."

Then the singing began.

The (Alleged) Harasser had begun to sing along with the cassettes. According to the Witness, it was a high, piercing, yet oddly toneless vocalization, described as "the whistles of a deflating prophylactic." Even then, that vocal component, not lacking in enthusiasm., might have been bearable had the individual then not insisted all present join in. Then, after a few weeks, the gingerbread men.

These cookies consisted of brown sugar, flour, baking soda, cinnamon, ginger, cloves, salt, butter, milk, and molasses. The ratio of molasses and brown sugar to flour is fairly high, the Witness asserted, and as a result, while retaining candied features, they were fairly deformed, he said, really more like "crusty, beady eyed butt plugs" than anything else. The (Alleged) Harasser would also show up at the Symphony offices while the Witness was in meetings with Receptionist Kenan Schucks and leave the cookies at the front desk. This individual has also physically stepped into the Men's Dressing Room Area and whispered in the Witness's ear when walking past the door. The Witness reported that the (Alleged) Harasser's pattern of singing and leaving gingerbread men escalated in February to multiple times daily. The Witness reported that she said she liked to hand out gingerbread men indiscriminately, whether the recipient had been "naughty" or "nice." For example, she'd drop off a gingerbread man when he arrived at rehearsals and to say good-bye before he left. Said Witness stated that the cookies were "virtually inedible" and that he felt the ginger and salt in the back of his throat for several minutes after swallowing.

"I felt violated," he stated.

Then, in October of 2013, the Witness walked back down to the green room after meeting with the music director Michel Butrie. He said that as he sat down, he could see something taped onto the mirror above his chair. As he moved closer, he was then able to identify what it was: a decaying sprig of mistletoe. He could also see the lid of his English horn case was not the way he had left it; it was ajar. In the adjoining dressing room area where he knew she had set up her cassette player, through the walls, he could hear the music begin again. The Witness stated that he then took a deep breath, opened the case, and looked inside. He then went to the restroom and cried: another of the (Alleged) Harasser's gingerbread men had been placed in his own personal effects on top of photos he keeps inside the case, including one of the Stonehaven Symphony receptionist he identifies as his significant life partner. Hanging out of its mouth, an enormous red Pull 'N' Peel Twizzler.

Voice No. 2: (Beatrice Sara?) Make my wish come true!

Voice No. 1: (Fatima.) Um, yes. Of course, whatever, if that is what you wish, Miss Sara. I know you're one of the judges on the clarinet audition panel next week…

Voice No. 2: (with a creepy, sing-songy voice): Oh, I just want you for my own. More than you could ever know.

Voice No. 1: Yes, that's so funny. But can you tell me how I play the section here, please…

Voice No. 2: (with higher voice) This is all I'm asking for!

Voice No. 1: Yes. Um, maybe I should go now.

Voice No. 2: Just relax! Fatima! How do you relax in your culture? I never asked you where your family comes from… do your people smoke anything?

Voice No. 1: Pittsburgh.

Voice No. 2: Hang on. Give me a sec, I got my scented candle right here and here's a match… there, hope it doesn't trigger the sprinklers! Okay, now, isn't that better? Just breathe it in. Breathe it out. Hmmm. Now, let's just go back to bar 15.

(Clarinet hesitantly plays some notes, possibly Tchaikovsky, possibly Li'l Skank, pretty out of tune.)

Voice No. 2: Okay, okay! But now try playing it just like how she sings. So powerful, with those effortless high notes. Here, let me rewind the tape, and we can listen a few more times...

(Clarinet suddenly begins to play what may have been the same pitches like an electric cattle prod had been applied, perhaps internally.)

Voice No. 2: My goodness, Fatima! I've never heard a bass clarinet do that before. Why don't you take a moment to screw it back together now. Are you okay? Alright, see, that's better already. Wow, Fatima, you did great! That was fire! How does it feel?

Voice No. 1: I feel dirty.

Voice No. 2: Listen to me, Fatima! We've got plenty of time. And it's almost December, so you know what that means! Maybe if we just sing your lines together...

Voice No. 1: Oh, please, no. No more singing, Miss Sara. I think I'll be okay on my own now...

Wittner Metronome

Carrie Marie Season Scented Candle

Holiday Sweater (womens xx-large)

Red Hat (plush, white pom-pom balls, green jagged trim, velcro tabs)

(2) 5 Inch Rigid Contoured 100% Polyurethane Prosthetic Elf Ears

Candy Canes (assorted)

7 Inch Traditional Wooden Nutcracker Decoration

11 Piece 2 Inch Nativity Set (lighted)

Magnetic Hanukkah Travel Menorah

Hallmark Santa Claus is Comin' to Town Kris Kringle Ornament

Naughty and Nice Pajama Set

Holiday Nail Polish Set

Gemmy Inflatable Grinch

Carrie Marie – *Marie Christmas* (1994, audio cassette)

Summary of key evidence completed, I stood up and examined the photo on the cover of the cassette case, recognizing the angelic features of one of the most important musical visionaries of the late 20th Century. On the other end of the dressing table, the Tomashi player was still running with a cassette inside, but at the end of the tape.

I bent down and gently pried our orchestra librarian's fingers away from the large black garbage bag she had pulled over her head and gently removed it. A drama queen till the end. Then stepping over her body, I was able to reach the player and flip the cassette. Carrie Marie's *Like It's Christmas* immediately began to play. Lancy started twitching again, crying out for god's sake I am the personnel manager, I should do something, etc. Was able to restrain her with my foot before cranking up the volume.

As the voice of the 5-time Grammy winner, a Guinness World Record holder for the most Billboard Top 100 hits as a solo artist, filled the dressing room, time seemed to stand still.

It was 2005 and I was in college driving home from work. *Like It's Christmas* came on the radio. Carrie Marie changed my life.

BS   I know what you mean! For me. it was *Santa Claus is Coming to Town*.

YM   Listen, what's not to love? Carrie's got a set of pipes on her! Our Messiah soloists could only dream of those pipes. And the high notes on *Silent Night*?

BS   Like what was that? A high A?

YM   Yes, high A6! She's got fans all around the world who are in love with her, but it's only us musicians who can give her the full respect she deserves.

BS   She's totally the spirit of Christmas…

YM   After all she's been through in her life! The abuse! That ex-husband from Sony…

BS   And through it all, she keeps that Christmas spirit burning…

YM   I'll tell you what, if there's somebody who's gonna burn, it's that Hater. So controlling! And did you hear about how he was threatening her with a butter knife? A butter knife! I mean, Jesus Christ, she's vegan! .

BS   Amen, Yup.

YM You know, we go through our whole musical careers at this kind of mediocre level. The whole semi-pro orchestra thing. We tried to hire the best conductor we could get for the peanuts we can pay. And you, you're just trying to coach young, inexperienced musicians who want to audition for us, not so they can be transformed into great players, that's never what it's about, but just so they'll get the gig.

BS Well, Fatima's doing the best she can…

YM Real artists like Carrie are like the one chance they, most people, have, to get exposed to genius!

BS And holiday cheer!

YM … and now this hate is the reward you get! This is the way they're treating you!

BS Well, it's okay, but, Yup, just calm down, you're kind of scaring me. Breathe it in, breathe it out. I'm not really asking for anything. Sure, the whole gingerbread flour/salt ratio thing is kind of new to me…

YM We've got one chance to stand up for what's right in music. Once chance to show them, to show all those Haters! And smack that Sony guy in the mouth! We owe it to Carrie

---

A. *Background Information:* *Who are the people involved? Are they employees? Who reported and when? Attach more pages if necessary.*

1. Name of person who reported workplace harassment:

Harleen

2. If not the same person as above, name of person who allegedly experienced workplace harassment:

FatimaHashim

3. Attach more pages if necessary.

Lancy Headney, Stonehaven Symphony Music Librarian (decd.)

Wind subs (too many to mention)

Stonehaven High School side-by-side student musicians (ditto)

Ramon Gutierrez, Substitute Violin

4. Date complaint/concern raised and how:

Description of Facts

At 1835 hours on November 1, 2009. I, Stonehaven Symphony Orchestra Personnel Manager, Yup Michaels, was approached by Principal Viola Harleen Maris. Ambushed, really: she came out of the women's restroom behind me too quick for me to do much more than brace for impact. She was obviously agitated, again. She pulled me over to the woodwind dressing room door and said something like, "Yup, what do you hear in there?". I replied that I could hear a grown man crying. She said, "What about the noise? I replied that all I could hear was someone in the dressing room was playing a recording of Carrie Marie's incomparable *Jesus, Oh, What A Wonderful Child*. Harleen made an unpleasant face and said something like was that appropriate.

She then bodily yanked me around the corner to see Ramon Gutierrez. Ramon, the new violin sub from South America, was sitting on the floor in the prop room crying. I inquired as to what was wrong. Through tears, he said the music reminded him of his childhood. I immediately agreed with him, saying that I owed my formative years to Carrie Marie and that she had changed my young life.

Come to find out, Ramon's neighborhood in Panama was where U.S. forces laid siege to Manuel Noriega while broadcasting non-stop Christmas music at high volumes as psychological warfare.

Not knowing what to say to this, I did ask if it was from Carrie Marie's first or her revelatory second Christmas compilation. Before he could reply, I heard hysterical laughter from behind.

AP   Um, that would be Harles.

YM   So, Harleen Maris, Stonehaven Symphony Principal Viola?

AP   Yes.

YM   In other words, you personally never actually observed the harassment firsthand?

AP   Well, we all heard the screaming.

YM   Wait, you heard Fatima?

AP   Um, that was Harles.

YM   Harleen? Didn't you say she was outside in the parking lot?

AP   (nods) Yeah, she was pretty pissed off, too. Haven't seen her this mad since the Li'l Skank thing.

YM   Yes, sure, I remember her formal complaint. But do you have any idea what she saw that made her react like that?

AP   Don't think she's a big fan of Christmas. Or Carrie Marie.

YM   Not a fan of... Okay, can you repeat that last sentence for the record?

AP   Harleen's not a fan of Christmas.

YM   The last part.

AP   She hates Carrie Marie?

YM   She hates Carrie Marie.

AP   Well, that's Harles for you.

YM   She hates one of the most decorated vocalists of all time. She hates an artist who has literally changed people's lives. The only living woman with a pristine six-octave vocal range…

AP   I think so. She did say Carrie Marie sounds like when they spay goats.

YM   Oh. Oh, boy… Abby, has Harleen exhibited "unusual ideas, strange feelings, a lack of feelings, difficulty telling reality from fantasy, difficulty with self-care or a decline in personal hygiene"?

B. Investigation Plan: *You should plan and conduct the investigation. Attach more pages if necessary.*

1 An investigator needs to interview the Complainant and the (Alleged) Harasser.

(You're supposed to do it in that order too. Otherwise, you really have no idea what has been alleged about the harasser.)

2 Make a list of possible relevant witnesses.

(And make a list of key evidence. And any documents provided in the course of the investigation, and don't forget audio, video, and surveillance footage. Better make a list for everything, really.)

3   Interview relevant witnesses. Ask specific questions about what they have observed, are aware of or have personally experienced.

(But don't include hearsay. Especially if they have undereducated opinions about singers outside of their limited classical music expertise, like pop icons.)

Principle. *Interview techniques can facilitate witness memory and encourage communication both during and following the interview.*

Policy. *You should conduct a complete, efficient, and effective interview of the witness and encourage post interview communication.*

Procedure. *During the interview, don't forget to:*

1. Encourage the witness to volunteer information without prompting (e.g. I want to start out with some basic info…).

2. Encourage the witness to tell you all the details, even if they seem trivial.

3. Ask open-ended questions (e.g. What's a difference between a clarinet and a bassoon?) and augment with closed-ended, specific questions (e.g. Which one of the two would take longer to burn?).

4. Ask the witness to mentally recreate the circumstances of the event (e.g. Think about your feelings at the time.).

5. Express empathy at all times.

6. Develop note-taking shorthand for nonverbal behavior (i.e. every vocalization and gesture is critical inc. pauses, squinty eyes, involuntary movements, etc.)

HM   [////]

YM   Let's start with some basic info: *Have you ever* thought of harming yourself or trying to take your own life?

HM   [DB] Yup, this is not about me [!]

YM   Oh, no, of course it isn't, Harleen. Now, can you tell me all the details, even if they seem trivial?

HM   You sound like tech support. [DII] How are you even qualified to run an investigation, Yup? Are those note cards?

YM   Wait, what are you… Harleen, I need those! That's confidential information, all my interviews…

HM   [Lgh] Listen, first off, why are you questioning me? If you knew what you were doing, you'd be talking to Fatima or what's his name, Kenan's boyfriend. Anybody in the wind section… come to think of it, nobody in the whole wind section actually has a spine. But Yup, what kind of an orchestra allows this kind of harassment? With that noise going on during breaks? You can't even call that Carrie Marie stuff music. Yup, Christmas isn't for another four weeks! And then those cookies? {:0

YM   "How can you even… Carrie Marie… music." Wow. Okay. I have no words. But I'm okay. Uh, can you mentally recreate the taste of the cookie you mentioned…

HM   The gingerbread thing? It had a smell to it. It smelled funny.

YM   How did it taste?

HM   [(o)(o)] Taste? Who would put one of those ugly piles in their mouth? [DII] Revolting. You could see whoever baked it was developmentally disabled. The legs, just bulbous stubs. Mine had one eyeball. It was like, what is this supposed to be?

YM   Got it. Though you had mentioned they were anatomically correct...

HM   Well, sure, in a depraved way, [<~o o~>] [...] [CT] Yup, the cookie had testicles, [SIC] just gross...

YM   Yes, right, right. Listen, I am so sorry you had to go through this, Harleen. And I know it's difficult to relive this. You're a survivor. You rock. Do you need a tissue?

HM   [(o)(o)]

YM   But I have to ask you a sensitive follow up question: if your gingerbread man did not have legs, how can you be sure you were looking at testicles?

G. Investigation Result(s)

The investigator's summary report should set out who was interviewed, what evidence was obtained and an analysis of the evidence to determine whether workplace harassment occurred. Attach more pages if necessary.

I, Stonehaven Symphony Orchestra Personnel Manager, Yup Michaels, did investigate charges of "workplace harassment of a psychological nature involving hostile or unwanted behavior, attacks on dignity or well-being, as well as repetition and severity." In the process thereof, I have interviewed the Complainant, Harleen Maris, and the (Alleged) Harasser, Beatrice Sara. The process has been exacerbated by the unwillingness of a number of witnesses, who were themselves potential complainants, to formally register their complaints due to fear of (alleged) reprisal ("You better watch out, You better not cry, You better not pout, I'm telling you why"), despite my assurances.

However, upon further examination, the reliability of the Complainant and the Witnesses must be called into question as the result of a number of discrepancies that have come to light. Contradictions, irregularities, and incredulities that may well invalidate the whole point of this entire investigation procedure.

- Interview: Abigail Peck. Refused to press charges for fear of reprisal. (Note: to be fair, the Witness' concern of reprisal actually appear to involve a fear of the Complainant.)
- Witness Fatima Hashim. If Fatima had really been so traumatized by Bea's Christmas treats, why was she seen eating a Family Pack of red Pull 'N' Peel Twizzlers last week?
- Witness Ramon Gutierrez. There is also surveillance footage of Ramon sitting on the floor outside the dressing room crying after your Music of South America marathon last spring.
- That woodwind extra ("What's His Name") has already been removed from our sub list.
- Interview: Harleen Maris. Harleen. Need we say more?
- Autopsy Report: Lancy Headney. Well, she did have a history of Irritable Bowel Syndrome.

Investigator Signature: _____ Yup Michaels _____

Report provided to: _____ Maestro Michael Butrie _____

Date (dd/mm/yyyy): _____ 12/25/2012 _____

Possible Note Taking Shorthand for Nonverbal Behavior

[=>] Break of gaze to the right

[CT] Clear throat

[DB] Deep breath or sigh

[...] Delayed response

[e] Early response

[Grm] Grooming behavior

[!] Loud or emphasized

[Lgh] Laugh

[SIC] Shift in chair

[WP] Weeping

[UebG] Uncontrolled emission of bodily Gas

[mmm] Humming along with background music

[````] Air drumming

[Nif] Nervous instrument fingering

[/\ ] Practicing scales.

[bzzzz] Lip buzzing

[////] Foot tapping

[DII] Direct eye to eye contact

[o,,,,] Eye rolling

[<~o o~>] Shifty eyes

[(o)(o)] Deer in headlights, stunned

{:0 Hyperventilation

MUSICIANS DO CARE

Truman Boyd, SIFT Western Regional Orchestras Awards Panel Secretary

Paper Record, charred

2008

Did you know ticket sales alone cannot sustain a symphony orchestra?

When orchestra administrators are not courting donors or waiting for bequestors to die, grant funding is the name of the game. A remarkably well-preserved copy of an awards panel proceeding was found in the tour bus wreckage. It gives us a glimpse into the petty power struggles of so many such adjudications.

There is also a proposal for a program called Musicians Do Care. Musicians Do Care was a collection of several concert initiatives, including a new arrangement of Edvard Grieg's monumental Peer Gynt, but for puppet theater.

For the average person the story of Peer Gynt's journey from the Norwegian mountains to the deserts of Africa and back is pretty surreal. Now imagine what if such a person was plastered with navy strength rum espresso.

SIFT Western Regional Orchestras Awards Panel
Meeting Minutes
Sendler Library Conference Room

Present: Gay Feros, Chairwoman

                  Charlette Magne, President, Colorado Foundation for Fertility Research

                  Marc Sendler, CEO, Stonehaven Dumb Friends League

                  Melissa 'Elisa' Sendler, SIFT Chair Emeritus and Platinum Level SIFT Donor

                  Truman Boyd, Secretary

Regrets: Rodney Feros, Vice Chair

Guests: Yup Michaels, Stonehaven Symphony award applicant

PROCEEDINGS:

1. Call to Order. Gay Feros, Chairwoman, called the meeting to order at 7:04 pm.

    a) Marc Sendler inquired about Rodney Feros, Vice Chair, who was absent. Gay Feros said ask Charlotte. Charlotte said Rodney was looking good at the Stonehaven Symphony puppet show on Sunday. Marc started to cry. Condolences were offered to Sendler family. A moment of silence was requested. Marc thanked the panel and said his mother, Chair Emeritus Elisa Sendler, would have been grateful.

        i. Tissues were distributed.

2. Approval of December Minutes. Minutes were reviewed. Gay Feros, Chairwoman, called for a MOTION.

a) Gurgling noise from Elisa Sendler, Chair Emeritus.

b) Members of the Panel (Gay Feros excepted), previously unaware of the Chair Emeritus behind the copier, stood and gathered around expressing surprise and concern. Gay complimented this secretary on his tight new dress pants before admonishing him to "just sit down and keep up with the notes."

c) Gay called for a SECOND. Several discussions ensued. Gay pounded a large metal thermos on the table and called for order.

d) Discussion ceased. Marc Sendler made "the second thing". Seconded and passed.

3. Chairwoman's Report: Gay Feros, Chairwoman, noted the past three meetings have run over the intended two-hour time slot by half an hour. Everybody be more mindful and focused during discussions. Marc Sendler, as a SIFT development coordinator, was to remain vigilant of the time, take an action to identify solutions to this issue, and "grow a spine."

a) Marc tearfully apologized and requested permission to smoke a cigarette.

b) Permission denied.

c) Charlette Magne could be heard quietly comforting the Chair Emeritus.

i. She did express concern such that Gay Feros might presently be compromised by intimate issues of a marital nature.

d) Gay compared Charlotte's marital nature to that of a flying leech-like insect. She stated the Panel was not to focus on Elisa's condition. Move forward with the allocation of the monies the Chair Emeritus had graciously endowed in the event of her death or just such a vegetative state. That said, what the hell happened at the puppet show.

4. Application Review. Stonehaven Symphony co-applicant, Yup Michaels, approached the Panel. Yup read the organization's application statement.

   a) "American orchestras have had more than their usual share of strikes, lockouts, and bankruptcies, but the Stonehaven Symphony, under the superb leadership of Michel Butrie, Ph.D, is beginning to reverse this deficit trend line and at the same time engage our community with his brilliant new audience outreach initiative, Musicians Do Care™."

   b) Discussion: what to do with the Chair Emeritus, who was snoring. Yup appeared to be unsure of how or whether to proceed. Marc asked where was co-applicant Michel Butrie. Yup apologized on behalf of Michel who was unable to attend today and sadly indisposed "due to exhaustion".

      i. Chairwoman Gay Feros' thermos rolled to the floor. Several discussions ensued. Gay Feros advised this secretary that "Charlotte has that effect."

5. Subcommittee Review. Gay Feros, Chairwoman, called for the formal subcommittee review of the Symphony application, to be presented by Marc Sendler and Charlotte Magne.

   a) Charlotte recused herself and left the room at 7:26 pm, citing morning sickness.

   b) Marc stated that he was more comfortable in the field of animal husbandry and welfare due to his position as CEO of the Stonehaven Dumb Friends League.

        i. He also noted that he'd left to grab a smoke halfway through the puppet show.

c) "Musicians Do Care is a community engagement initiative of the Stonehaven Symphony that seeks to enhance the quality of life for people of all ages whose healthcare needs and/or criminal convictions prevent them from attending traditional music performances. We provide live, interactive musical experiences including an Instrument Petting Zoo, the Music for the Deaf, Deafened, and Hard of Hearing, and, of course, the Peer Gynt Puppet Show Gala. We musicians care deeply enough about our community that we no longer merely perform concerts: we "Do" our community. Music offers health benefits throughout life, from those born into the neonatal intensive care unit for whom music mediates medical stress, through those in hospice care at the end of life who can use the music to mitigate and mask the grotesque symptoms and declines of age (Marc motioned back toward his mother), to those who do have legal criminal convictions and deserve to be punished to the fullest extent of the law.

        i. Marc was cautioned to stop just reading the application verbatim. Marc noted that he didn't know what else to say. He was advised to evaluate musical performance and audience response.

        ii. Marc responded that both musicians and audience appeared well-groomed and fed.

d) A high-pitched sound interrupted the proceedings.

        i. Gay dropped the metal thermos she had prepared to hurl at Marc.

ii. Charlotte Magne returned at 7:27 pm.

iii. A brief recess was declared as Charlotte tried to roll the sleeping Chair Emeritus off the medical alert in her hand.

e) Charlotte was asked to evaluate the Musicians Do Care Instrument Petting Zoo program. Noting that as President of the Colorado Foundation for Fertility Research and a professional women's fertility advocate, she was by no means a musical expert, she explained that Stonehaven Symphony musicians introduce unwanted inner-city children ages 5-12 to orchestral music through a variety of age-appropriate activities, working with the youth to quell gang violence. These unwanted children have been left to the streets, even as hundreds of women around the state struggle to become inseminated every year.

Charlotte further detailed the assisted reproductive technology and sperm donation techniques often employed.

i. On behalf of the Panel, Gay expressed gratitude that there was one woman in Stonehaven who never had such struggles.

f) Marc added that activities include movement to music, soundscapes, rhythmic recognition, composition and the "instrument petting zoo," a popular hands-on format that allows children to hold and touch real musical instruments and musicians. He said Symphony musicians quickly become accustomed to these educational gropings. Yup Michaels confirmed that American orchestral musicians are always grateful for any kind of musical income, whatever the indignity.

Marc added that he will never forget one little boy's smiling face after he evidently snatched a 100- year-old cello from the hands of a musician and ran his stubby fingers through her hair, shouting, "Look who da pimp now!"

g) Gay Feros, Chairwoman, finally asked for this secretary's "manly" assistance unscrewing her thermos. She poured out the contents, then asked this secretary's opinion. This secretary was aware of a burning sensation.

   i. Laughter. Was not decaf. She said espresso and rum. Gay Feros and this secretary began to share the 30-ounce remainder.

h) Marc said he did feel like he could speak to the Musicians Do Care's Music for the Deaf, Deafened, and Hard of Hearing program, which was presented over in the lobby of Dumb Friends League building where he works.

   i. In October and February, the Symphony produced a total of six outreach events targeting hearing disabled adults and children. The project incorporated sign language interpretation, speech-to-text relay, and some kind of hand-held "transductional" speakers to increase accessibility as far as possible. Visitors were supposed to sit next the musicians while holding the vibrating devices, literally "feeling the music inside their bodies".

i) Yup Michaels provided examples which originated as an assignment for a remedial Stonehaven High School industrial arts class.

- i. The rubbery vegetable-like devices, which the high schoolers called "Tone Sausages," were passed around the table.
- j) The question was raised of what's the point trying to get deaf people to listen to music.
- k) Marc started talking about how animals face similar discriminatory attitudes.
  - i. In fact, he argued, deaf dogs are rising to the top of the A-list at shelters. It wasn't long ago that any animal coming into a shelter with a defect, be it three legs or one eye, was considered unadoptable and automatically destroyed. It was hard enough finding homes for the close-to-perfect animals that made their way through the doors, so most shelter staff didn't consider it worth the effort to promote animals with special needs. But deaf dogs are incredible. Sometimes, they pull off tremendous heroic and athletic feats. Deaf, one-eyed, three-legged, and even incontinent canines can live full happy lives, he said. Just spend some time with one, and you'll see how much they can enjoy a wide range of activities and certainly can give just as much love as any pet. He said they simply adapt and frolic on.
- l) A disturbing bowel sound interrupted the proceedings. The Chair Emeritus had grown restless. Recess was declared.
  - i. Three vibrating Tone Sausages were discovered in the gurney and destroyed. The bed pan in question, disposed of.

m) Yup Michaels insisted Elisa looked fine when Charlotte and Rodney Feros had rolled her into the Sendler Library Sunday afternoon.

    i. He went on about how since 2007, assisted living facilities have been enchanted by puppet shows that feature timeless stories supported by classical music geared for AARP ages 55 on up. Prior to the 20-minute performance, facilities receive a curriculum kit that includes a CD of music and narrative, a story synopsis, finger puppet art work to be copied for the elderly to color and assemble, and laminated posters of characters.

6. The Puppet Show. 19th century Norwegian composer Edvard Grieg's *Peer Gynt* was mounted by a dedicated group of six puppeteers on a miniature stage involving sets, props, lighting, and delightful puppet characters, accompanied by our very own Stonehaven Symphony musicians.

    i. Yup Michaels also provided examples of the puppets, which originated as extra-credit for the same remedial Stonehaven High School industrial arts class.

    ii. The Chair Emeritus became agitated when she recognized the crudely painted sock figures. Marc requested that they be put "far away".

    iii. Gay's speech became somewhat slurred. Didn't understand how her husband was even at the puppet show. Was supposed to be home cleaning the garage.

    iv. What was he doing with Charlotte?

v. Charlotte observed that in the puppet show, Peer Gynt is a poet and a braggart, but otherwise a pretty good-looking guy from the village of Kvam in Gudbrandsdalen. Peer is banished for kidnapping the Ingrid from her wedding, which should have been a joyous, empowering life event. Later he wanders the mountains and meets three dairymaids who were waiting for trolls, which, Charlotte clarified, were the mythological equivalent of egg donors. She explained it was only natural that these young women would seek an alternative to the Kvam townsmen, many of whom exhibited histories or evidence of alcohol or drug abuse, negative behavioral characteristics, manic depressive illness or schizophrenia, and inbreeding. Charlette explained that she herself had been more interested in certain donor attributes.

vi. She listed "tall," "smart," "very good at math (because I'm more of a words person)," "musical," and "brown haired".

vii. Gay reiterated her desire to know what the hell happened at the puppet show.

viii. Charlotte said Yup and Marc had been sitting right next to Chair Emeritus at the performance. It was probably about the time in the story that Peer had become highly intoxicated with the dairymaids and run head-first into a rock before losing consciousness.

ix. According to Yup Michaels, the Chair Emeritus had remarked that the puppet was the lucky one.

x. Marc added that after Rodney and Charlotte had left her in the front row to visit the library's new family restroom together, his mother indeed looked like a trapped rescue animal. And that was before Peer Gynt left the troll witch and came across the Green Hilda puppet who claimed to be the daughter of Dovregubben, the troll mountain king.

    I. The next part, Marc stated, was pretty explicit for a puppet show.

    II. "After that, even I needed a cigarette."

    III. Gay Feros, Chairwoman, clung to this secretary's elbow and asked "Is this really happening?"

xi. Marc described how as he strode out of the community room, he could still hear the little puppet denying that he inseminated Green Hilda. Unmoved, the Mountain King Dovregubben sat on his throne in the great hall, with crown and sceptre, surrounded by his children and relatives there amidst the great puppet crowd of trollcourtiers, gnomes and goblins.

xii. Marc appeared to be distraught again.

xiii. The wise troll king replied that Peer begat Green Hilda's child in his head.

xiv. Charlotte explained that this could have been one of the earliest cases of intercervical conception. She clarified that sperm banks do set limits on the number of offspring a donor is allowed to have before they cut them from the program. She had personally tried to convince herself that she didn't care about this number, but realized that, overall, it really did bother her.

xv. As she explained to Michel Butrie in his dressing room after the performance, even today, women recognize that there is a high likelihood that their children will have a couple of half-siblings out there, but "a girl's gotta do what a girl's gotta do."

xvi. Vice-Chair Rodney Feros suddenly stood up from behind the potted plant by the door, expressing disappointment that Charlette had disappeared into Michel Butrie's dressing room after the puppet show.

xvii. Gay Feros compared her husband's marital nature to that of a neutered beast of burden.

xviii. Charlotte again recused herself and left the room at 8:03 pm citing morning sickness.

xix. Marc said he was reminded of the fact that every year, approximately 1.5 million animals are euthanized (670,00 dogs and 860,000 cats).

xx. Rodney did question as to why was his wife "hanging on Truman's arm like a witch in heat."

    I. Gay released this secretary's elbow and slid off her chair onto the floor.

    II. Marc said he could still see his mother sitting on her throne with crown and sceptre, begging him not to leave her there.

III.   He mentioned that of the dogs entering shelters, approximately 48% are adopted and 20% are euthanized. Of the cats entering shelters, approximately 50% are adopted and 27% are euthanized (or, as this secretary was becoming somewhat inebriated, possibly the other way around).

IV.   Marc began to weep openly.

V.   He proceeded to light the cigarette still in his hand. Chairwoman Gay Feros could be heard expressing disapproval under the conference table. Unable to find a place to put it out, Marc agitatedly dropped it into Gay's nearly empty thermos, where it came into contact with the 151-proof residue, and the conference table was engulfed in flames.

VI.   Troll courtiers, gnomes, and goblins leapt from their chairs and screamed and danced, trying to retrieve personal electronics and Gay Feros.

xxi.   Green Hilda entered the great hall at 8:03 pm, citing morning sickness.

i.   This secretary finally threw himself across the table and attempted to smother the flames with a spare puppet.

7. Behind the Copier. Dovregubben suddenly sat bolt upright in her gurney and remarked, "Doesn't he have a nice ass?"

    a) Three dairymaids defended the orchestra's application with 19th Century Norwegian composer Edvard Grieg's own words.

        i. "For the Hall of the Mountain King I have written something that so reeks of cowpats, ultra-Norwegianism, and 'to-thyself-be-enough-ness' that I can't bear to hear it, though I hope that the irony will make itself felt."

8. Adjournment. Dovregubben made a MOTION to adjourn the meeting. Green Hilda seconded the motion. The motion passed and meeting was adjourned at 8:39 pm.

Respectfully Submitted,

Peer Gynt

HAUTE PLAINS DRIFTER

> **Haute Plains Drifter**
>
> Author Unknown
>
> *Linen Stationary, scented*
>
> *2013*
>
> *Living composers are the bane of a conductor's existence. Demanding, unscrupulous, often dishonest, they will do anything to hear their music performed. Of course, conductors know full well their audiences would much rather hear Mozart and Beethoven over and over again. These letters, violently crumpled, were retrieved from a waste basket in the Stonehaven Symphony's tour bus aft cabin. They chronicle the solicitations of one such young composer, whose real name we may never know, as well the consequences of even giving him the time of day.*

4 March

to Maestro Michel Butrie:

i hope you will excuse the liberty i have taken in writing these few lines hoping this will find you in good health as is my family at present. how are you this fine Spring day? perhaps you remember me. my mother,

Suzie Eckstein, spoke with you at the Stonehaven Symphony Gala last week. peering over the punch bowl, an unremarkable woman in her eighties, octangular glasses, white hair tufted around a feathered hat? like the very bird so deprived, perhaps not the most sparkling example of intellect. not even i am so impressed, and she is, as i've said, my mother! then again my childhood was an abusive house of horrors she would no doubt deny, stories for another day. but beneath the volucrine façade, her very presence at the Gala, like great music, lies in a value beyond such moral judgments. above mere blatherings of right and wrong and good and evil. though inseparable from the Endowment our family has lavished upon your Conductor's Chair.

but did she mention that the Endowment of Music burns within me as well? of course, she didn't! well as a child, after my untimely expulsion from the Denver School of the Arts, i was finally free to plumb my passions. Sculpture, poetry, Zen Kabuki Theatre, Krav Maga, all while travelling the globe -- and France, ah, *Française*! as a young man in search of i know not what. but none captured my imagination so much as the simple act of writing orchestral concertos. big ones, little ones, fast ones, slow ones. like wild dreams—but dreams i want to realize. life and literature combined, loving the dynamo... my Professeur Camille de Craveau knew this. he would draw his Denver School of the Arts music colleagues aside. together they would discuss my weekly counterpoint exercises in various tongues, searching for the words. indeed, that is how i came to be known as *Le Freak*.

Mais c'est vrai, my mother had perhaps a little too much to drink. her words only forgivable, or at least sufferable, when taking into consideration her said importance to the organization, see above. why, just as you, a visionary music director, hold considerable importance in your own way, and influence over symphonic programming. except she perhaps more so, given the sad financial outcome of the Symphony Gala. but then after all the donations our family has made on behalf of the Symphony, i believe i overheard her to say, "My husband and I could have sent Freddie to Yale with the money we spent on you. now, no more of that modern music *gärbij* at the concerts, young man. Or you will be flipping the burgers!"

was i ashamed of her for saying such? *Bien sûr.* yet there i stood, just within earshot off to the side, listening intently. yes, that was i, the tall, bearded ruggedly-handsome young man perhaps slightly unkempt after a week hitchhiking, with hand over mouth of the suspicious *maître d'*.

why did i not take that opportunity to introduce myself then and there? why did she never once acknowledge my own presence? it is true that years of abuse -- sometimes sexual in nature -- has put a damper on our relationship. i've been left scarred, damaged, something of an introvert. a tortured artist. but, as it turns out, a composer of avant-garde musical compositions! in the grand tradition of Arnold Schoenberg, Karlheinz Stockhausen, and the immortal Igor Stravinsky.

Igor. *Igor, Igor, Igor!* even the name itself conjures wild visions of unbridled creativity and Bacchanalian mastery! forgive me – for i feel on a first name basis. how that man speaks to me.

but enough about me. i understand you are soon to announce the upcoming season. please tell me we won't be hearing more of those long Mahler yawners. the last thing Stonehaven audiences need is to be bored.

but imagine, if you will, what would happen if you programmed a new work, a world premiere composed by a young composer with local connections. yes, Michel (if i may be so bold), i refer to myself, for i have just the piece in mind! imagine the public response and recognition that would then be yours! imagine the sight and significance of an old woman's smile. imagine if that old woman was Mother and the financial significance therein.

don't expect me to be sane anymore. don't let's be sensible. we must discuss this exciting prospect at length and at your earliest convenience.

i await your enthusiasm,

Ton frere en musique,

Frederick ("Freddie") Eckstein

Composer/Author/*Freak*

7 March

ah, Maestro,

this afternoon i arrived for our meeting, 8:00 am sharp. i do not know how to express or analyze the conflicting emotions that have surged like a storm through my heart when the new guy (Kevin?) told me you were indisposed! i composed a more beautiful letter to you than this in the sleepless nightmare hours of the night. this is all that remains: *i am reduced to a thing that wants Michel. i just miss you, in a quite simple desperate human way. i feel somehow that it is a disgrace to do nothing, to just bide one's time, to take it philosophically, to be sensible. i read the paper about suicides and murders, and i understand it all thoroughly. i feel suicidal... murderous.*

come to find out, Kevin loves being the orchestra receptionist. he loves his new desk and floor lamp and pink Scotch tape dispenser. he is nothing if not devoted to your organization. i choked back the tears and explained who i was. he repeated: you left a message saying you were indisposed. with sincerest regrets. deepest apologies.

i said that's fine, thank you very much. i'll wait.

we watched the dappled light move across your office door as the sun crawled through the trees outside the window. Michel, you can learn a lot about somebody after five hours. did you know Kenan loves reggae music, long walks, and scented body paint? Eventually, he was apologizing on behalf of the organization, complimenting my toned physique, asking if there was anything he could do to make it up to me, anything at all, and yada yada.

but such a hale and hearty fellow such as yourself? at home with a cold? I freely offered of my skepticism. after all, when i finally left Kenan Scotch-taped to the lamp and walked back outside, i could see your Prius in the parking lot. right where i'd chalked the tires yesterday. for a moment, i feared all was lost. but our stars aligned once again: your office window was ajar!

with a boost from a symphony audition finalist i discovered shooting up in the hedge below, i grabbed the sill. from there, it was just a question of prying the glass the rest of the way open and shimmying through on my belly. i passed that night in your office, admiring your extensive collection of color-coded rehearsal sticky notes as well as one of the most well-stocked portable refrigerators i've personally ever experienced before passing out. while it thundered and lightninged i lay naked on your desk and went through wild dreams. you and i were in Seville and then in Fez and then in Capri and then in Havana. we are journeying constantly, but there is always a baton and musical scores, and your face is always close to mine and the look in your eyes never changes.

i was as surprised as you this morning when you finally opened the door. silly me, half-asleep, sprawled out across your desk like the morgue scene from Piazzolla's *María de Buenos Aires*. but surprise, even abject horror, has its limits. after i reminded you my mother's financial generosity also has its limits, you finally stopped screaming.

it is true that my years of molestation at Mother's hands have been something of a family secret. that being why your orchestra manager (Yup Michaels?) told you she's never mentioned me. so he's threatened to phone her tomorrow? well, of course, if you were to ask her, she would deny everything. that would be awkward. i wouldn't.

the point is that then and only then you and i were able to have a real discourse, artist to artist, composer to interpreter. like the great Manuel

DeFalla to whoever his conductor was. we spoke of many things -- the wild dream i want to realize, of life and music combined, the dynamo, you with your asexual lizard soul birthing me dozens of musicians, while anchored always in no matter what storm, the pineal eye of my hallucinations:

we spoke of the orchestral concerto i shall compose.

inspired during a recent pharmaceutical transaction in Tijuana, i have conceived of a major concerto for orchestra! sure to enflame the local populace in general, in particular those of Hispanic persuasion, it is based on the noble Spanish army's arrival in Mexico in the year 1520. you did have reservations with regard to my working title, *Massacre in the Great Temple of Tenochtitlan*. but, with the firm understanding i retain the work's story line, we settled upon your compromise, *Spanish Dances*. forgive me if i take this moment to pass gas.

i shall commence my labors heretofore. do not worry the Muse will abandon me before our appointed deadline for She and i have a deep understanding, born of years of intimacy. i dare say She fairly fears me. do not concern yourself with my commission fee. the faces of all those trapped under your baton shall be my sweet compensation. i shall release my inner Igor.

in the words of the great Tenochtitlan,

Oquichtli!

Fridrik Eckstein

Bon Vivant/muse/Ego Extraordinaire

8 March

my dearest Michel,

the expression on your own face, the trembling of your hands, the labored breathing, all upon seeing the long-awaited masterwork—it all exceeded my expectations. when you set the score down upon your desk and i told you the program had already been approved by the Symphony board, you seemed at a loss for words. at length, your lips began to move.

How, you asked, could i have written a 90-minute tone poem for enlarged symphony orchestra in the space of only 24 hours? Mozart, you groaned, Mozart could not have done such a thing!

well, i humbly responded, Mozart had not yet mastered the aleatoric arts. after all, the avant-garde technique of closing the eyes and scribbling random instructions for the musicians was not fully explored until my own lifetime, and even then, largely within the confines of asylums and penal colonies (there again, a story for another day).

there was the surprise of our new title, *A Day in the Life of the Spanish Fly*. you weren't any more enthusiastic about the title's inspired eroticism than the prospect of having to coordinate with the Yeshiva Boys' Choir. when you told the rabbi that the boys are to represent the famed Virgins of Tenochtitlan, he reported you to UNICEF.

how did you get reported to UNICEF for the grooming of underaged boys? you didn't think that was even a thing. but sure enough, the New York headquarters deployed their Emergency Response Team to establish a field presence at the Symphony offices. this morning, they detained you for a few questions. the psychological profile was fascinating: "Predator exposed to music as a child." "Genuinely believes he is a musical 'expert.'" "Recurrent, intense, arousing fantasies, urges and behaviors associated with musical performance and livestock." i didn't necessarily agree chemical castration was a good option, but in a way, i'm glad these findings mysteriously got leaked to the *Pioneer Gazette*, so the Stonehaven community can decide for itself. on a positive note, you did get a free Ebola shot. come to think of it, maybe i'll find another title.

but you asked where i expected you find to nine banjo players. i know you shall do what is necessary, for in the movement entitled *Patio of the Gods*, these humble Appalachian inbreds symbolize the arrival of the Spaniards. why, you asked, for what reason do we need banjos to represent those of Spanish descent? well, my simple friend, that's the enigmatic beauty of the instrument: there's really never a good reason for a banjo, is there?

you begged me, what would my dear old mother think of lasers and a fog machine in the *Grand Finale*? then started going on about how you didn't even know if i really was her son -- Yup did some digging around and says i'm making the whole thing up. he says this is all a case of attempted identity theft: Suzie Eckstein doesn't even have a son! come to find out she has a grown <u>daughter</u> named Freddie!!

well, yada yada. leave it to Yup to reinforce his own sexist gender stereotypes:

Suzie Eckstein <u>had</u> a daughter. the surgery was a success. now she has me.

screw her, the point is, we are on a conceptual journey, a holy quest to create new sonic worlds. it will not be easy. that night, we churned through the possibilities. you begged me to stop. yet in the mornings, continuing where we left off. resurrection after resurrection. you asserting yourself, begging for mercy; and the more you assert yourself the more you want me, need me. your voice getting hoarser, deeper, your eyes blacker, your blood thicker, your body fuller. a voluptuous servility and tyrannical necessity. more cruel now than before—consciously, willfully cruel. the insatiable delight of experience. what will tomorrow bring?

i clasp you cordially,

Freddi

They/Them/Theirs

3 May

Maestro, my maestro,

like the full-throated squeal of a newborn, our dress rehearsal of the newly-retitled *Conquistador, Mon Amour* echoed through Slope Auditorium. or were those the cries of your second violin section upon learning the entire 40-minute final movement is to be played *il più rapidamente possibile* on the G-string? an ingenious solution on my part, i must say, as that allows time for the brass, who were blowing lip-splitting high notes as loudly as possible during the prior six movements to pause, reflect, and see if they can still feel their faces. *Prego*! worry not, the musicians will come to accept, or at least endure, that which is their lot. it's in their nature. where else will they get paid? though in view of that, it probably was not a good time to remind them that since this is to be a benefit concert, they actually won't be getting paid.

of course, the banjo players are used to it. i hope you don't mind that i had to give the viola section a little pep talk. your principle, Harleen What's-Her-Name, certainly did. fortunately, after she made some snide remark about the rhythms in her solo not adding up, i was able to silence her by transposing her solo an octave up into treble clef on the spot. no such luck with your bassoonist, Miss Peck—what a spicy treat she is! oh, the lady doth protest too much, did she not? quoting union regulations, quite the earful. of course, i did what any composer would do (if he owned the orchestra... as Mother does)... i grabbed Miss Peck by the embouchure and dragged her out back. then i unzipped my ragged edition of Bartolozzi's *New Sounds for Woodwind* to page 39. If that doesn't teach her how to make wounded duck sounds on her bassoon, nothing will.

madness, you say? don't expect me to be sane anymore. don't let's be sensible. we are a marriage of allegiance, un ménage à trois—you, me, Mother, you can't dispute it. i came away from the rehearsal with pieces of you sticking to me; i am walking about, swimming, in an ocean of blood, your Canadian blood, distilled and gelatinous. i saw you as the mistress of your orchestra, a Nova Scotia Eskimo with a heavy face, a negress with a white body, eyes all over your skin, woman, woman, woman. i can't see how we can let the orchestra go at 10 pm—these intermissions are death. how did it seem to you when you went back to your home? was i still there? i can't picture you moving about with your rental car through your garage as you did with me. legs closed. frailty. sweet, treacherous acquiescence. bird docility. you became a man with my score. i was almost terrified by it. you are not just thirty years old— you are a Thousand!

that said, if i had one concern, it would be the Movement VII. i'm sensing a certain lack of conviction in the brass section. i understand some were still on their knees hyperventilating, but clearly they're going to need to pull themselves together before the final *tutti*. i notated very specific instructions for your Assistant Principle Horn, Parker DeVon: walk over to the podium and assemble the hibachi grill kit next to where Kenan rigged the fog machine. nowhere in the score does it say anything about him tearfully whispering to your union steward. i appreciate his artistic imagination, but no. *No.* he is the musician. i am the composer. he is the lamb. i am the slaughter

ah, but may you be the most magnificent cut of them all. no fear, for me it is all a symphonic feast, and I am so insatiable in living - God, Michel, in you alone i have found the same engorgement of enthusiasm, the same quick rising of the blood, the fullness... before, i almost used to think there was something wrong. Everybody else seemed to have napkins... i never feel the napkins. i dribble. and when i feel your excitement about music engorged, next to mine, well, it makes me flatulent.

until tomorrow i remain Your,

'Ryk

4 May

my noble incomparable Michel,

i am better at dry sadness than at cold anger, for i remained dry-eyed until now, as dry as smoked mutton, but my heart is a kind of dirty soft custard inside. but i am not sad. rather stunned, very far away from myself, not really believing you are now so far, so far. i want to tell you only three things before leaving town, and then i'll not speak about it anymore, i promise.

first, i really don't know what happened to the Yeshiva Boys Choir. i mean, obviously they caught on fire.

second, yes, guilty as charged: the first you heard of my title change was standing there beside me on stage at the concert as the audience started to murmur, not sure whether it was a joke. "*Montezuma's Revenge* for Symphony Orchestra" is a bit edgy, but then so is the true story of how the conquistadors entered the Great Temple that fateful day. the opening brass fanfare captured it perfectly. and you know the place where the tubas are instructed to turn around toward the percussion section and play *più fortissimo possible*? when your bongo player passed out? surely you read the program notes i distributed to the audience before you arrived. no matter—that's where the Spaniards storm the Aztec fiesta and cut the drummers' arms off.

your trumpet player, Pedro, had his instructions, which he executed to perfection. he symbolized Conquistadors encircling the hapless Aztecs. slowly, he walked through the auditorium seats, silently fingering *La Cucaracha* on his trumpet and locking all the doors. good thing, too, because a number of your older patrons looked like they had had enough. gathering their hearing aids and walkers, stumbling over each other (and your marketing team), just trying to get out of the auditorium. but it was the orchestra that really wanted out. maybe they didn't think my notated instructions made sense, or care if they lost their jobs. maybe they were still skeptical after the second violins finished grilling that rabbit in Movement VIII. believe it or not, it was actually my intention that Miss Peck begin weeping uncontrollably so the wind section would help her off the stage. after all, the beginning of the *Grand Finale* represents how the Conquistadors emerged from the evening mist and according to contemporaneous accounts *"struck some in the thighs and some in the calves. They slashed others in the abdomen and their entrails fell to the earth. There were some who even ran in vain, but their bowels spilled as they ran; they seemed to get their feet entangled with their own entrails."*

obviously, a lot for a young composer to represent with a single music composition. accidents happen. how could Kenan have known the fog machine was filled with red spray paint?

while it thundered and lightninged in my head, i lay on the floor backstage and went through wild dreams. we're in Seville and then in Fez and then in Capri and then in Havana. we're journeying constantly, but there is always a machine and books, and your baton is always close to me. it was a lot to memorize, but the dream never changes. people are saying we will be miserable, we will regret, but we are happy, we are laughing always, we are singing, *"I-gor, I-gor, I-gooooor!"* we are talking Spanish and French and Arabic and *Türkçe*. we are admitted everywhere, and they strew our path with flowers.

also, it's true (as Yup so perceptively insisted), Suzie Eckstein is not my real mother. but no real mother of mine would have such a vindictive attitude toward contemporary music—or the conductors who program it. you must admit, she does possess that uber-mother vibe. *"Who are you?"* you finally screamed as i poked my head out the side curtains, our last chord together met with silence and distant fire engines. and yes, that does mean that Eckstein is not my real name, though surely the two of those, going hand in hand, only qualify as one thing.

i hope so much, i want and need so much to see you program my music again, some day. but, *remember, please* i shall never more *ask* you—not from any pride since i have none with you, as you know, but our music will mean something only when you wish it. so, i'll wait. when you'll wish it, just tell. i shall not assume that you have interest in my career anew, not even that you have to commission me, and we have not to commune for such a long time — just as you feel, and when you feel. but know that i'll always long for your asking me to compose for you. no, i cannot think that i shall not see you conduct my music again. i have lost your respect, and it was (it is) painful, but i shall not lose the memory of our time together, *your tearful face*, and the memory that spray paint is flammable.

and that more enjoyment of what remains of your artistry, your reputation, and your dignity, is still reserved for, dear Maestro, your most affectionate, &c.,

the man with no name

THE VISITORS

Welcome one, welcome all, to the Hausdermusik das Klangmuseum of Vienna.

We continually seek to improve the standard of the Hausdermusik galleries. To help accomplish this we are seeking the views of visitors to the Tutamen's Curse of the Maestro™ touring exhibition.

We also reserve a special 'das Willkommen' for our guests, the World Federation of Musicians' Colorado Pensioner Delegation. It is truly an honour to host so many familiar friends, who have come from so far, having endured so much.

We would be grateful if you could spend 4 or 5 minutes answering some questions here at our Museum Guestbook Kiosk.

1. *Select:*

> *Deutsch*
> *Italiano*
> *Francais*
> *English*

2. *Which words would you use to describe this exhibit in general? (Select one or more)*

> *informative*
> *fun*
> *exciting*
> *relevant*
> *cheerful*
> *good for kids*
> *didn't understand*

3. *Other words?*

> bizarre
> messed up
> American
> don't miss this place
> something for everyone if they're retired and over 70
> great for a rainy day when there's absolutely nothing else to do
> need more bathrooms
> Ewe!

4. *How did you hear about the Tutamen's Curse of the Maestro™ ? (Select)*

    Print Advertisement
    Poster
    Recommendation from someone
    Internet

5. *Other?*

    Vienna Times
    Eastern Slope Pioneer Gazette
    World Federation of Musicians newsletter
    therapist
    Aryan Hope Singles website

6. *How easy was it to understand the labels with the objects?*

  Everything was well-labelled. I especially enjoyed the high-resolution satellite images of the 2018 Stonehaven Symphony tour bus excavation.

  No other kind of music ever got near the intelligence and the courage of the symphony orchestra and its musicians. People in the United States think that everything started with those rappers. No, no, no, they were here because of Beethoven. Let's stop thinking that the United States and Great Britain have the answer to everything. It all started with classical composers that believed in GOD.

  i was completely taken by this deceptively small, disorganized exhibit. from the early description of Colorado's Stonehaven Symphony as "the orchestra of harmony" i was drawn in to the collection's engorged fullness—the way it captured the world of those obedient, simple-minded musicians, their manager "Yup" Michaels and that animal-loving Maestro Michel Butrie, a microcosm for today's wacky wonderful music industry. my faith restored, and my spirit cleansed.

Too bad the poor orchestra that caught on fire cannot be here to see us! But I guess if they were still alive, we wouldn't have this GREAT museum!! :)

No persons survived the accident? The bus just had a few indentations. We are so confused.

Could have done w/o the life-size sheep puppit.

Those were the woodwind players, not brass (mislabeled autopsy pics).

7. What, if anything, do you find particularly attractive or appealing about the exhibition?

What, if anything, is appealing about the fiery deaths of 50 co-workers?

Did not expect the interactive peyote kiosk.

That tour guide had a slightly mocking and negative tone of the classical music snobs.

This was totally Yup's bad. Dude thought he knew the way to Carnegie Hall. He was trippin.

POSITIVE: This is perhaps the first exhibition in this city in ca. 20 years which portrays the Western Music (i.e. White, European, etc.) in a "positive" – albeit neutral, quasi-uninformed manner (and not in "evil, destructive, oppressor" light)… it's about time! NEGATIVE: The Day in the Life of a Conductor video leaves the viewer with largely one of two impressions: either the conductor of the Stonehaven Symphony did little more than go on extended ego trips, or the curators had so little knowledge/interest in the positive cultural impact of symphonic activity that they did not or (perhaps were academically unable/unfit?) could not convey in words (more kiosks, please!) its significance.

Come to find out, Carnegie Hall is in New York. There isn't really an exit in Colorado.

How do you get to Carnegie Hall? Practice, practice, practice!

The regional orchestra musicians' living conditions brought me back to my own childhood busking in the slums of Beirut and Mogadishu after the coup.

I really liked Fiddle Mutton. I think he made everything funny. Because after a while it all got kind of sad!! :)

I don't get classical musicians. It was nice to sit down for the video. There's a goat in my backyard that stinks. It can't come in the house.

I think that it shows the Symphony didn't die in vain. They were trying to get to Carnegie Hall. That is what GOD wants for every musician. Then, their personnel manager drove off a cliff.

Nobody knew it was peyote. Crowley said it was cold medicine.

8. *Thinking of the Museum as a whole, how would you rate design and layout?*

Why is there no sign for the toilits or even exit signs? 12 minutes of my life I'll never get back.

The displays were pathetic; one screen show and very short slide show. That monitor won't show pictures full screen. The Sex Life of a Conductor diorama was pointless. You should put captions on all four sides of the cases to avoid traffic jams. Signage on embalmed livestock lacks explanations.

Hilarious German-English translations: "the sheep did play obediently for their Maestro"

I got to pee.. Where you put the bathrooms??

the more i listen to Beethoven the more i appreciate Igor Stravinsky. you know, i chatted up an American in Amsterdam. she wanted to me to dominate her at the symphony. we made sweet love in the balcony.

Marvelous. Old people (myself) could use more benches, particularly at mummified Stonehaven Symphony Cello Section remains. Magnifying glasses were great. Thanks.

9. How did the Stonehaven Symphony's treatment of its musicians make you feel?

This is pretty inappropriate. Especially the eyewitness accounts of rescue workers arriving at the scene and smelling roast kebob.

Beautiful artifacts, very rich and informative. But, no references to the ugly side of symphonic expansion in the U.S.: slavery, disease, death, colonization. The history's whitewashed.

Bravo! I was impressed by the beautiful and varied instruments presented in the exhibition. However, like one of the visitor's comments on the previous page, I was disappointed by the fact that no mention was made of the contribution by Nazis to the development of the modern orchestra. Unfortunately, Colorado seems to give short shrift to this part of its history, just as it unfailingly avoids mention of the terrible chapter of the 2007 Stonehaven Symphony Concert of Contemporary Music. Perhaps now that Colorado is emerging from its lethargy and truly entering the "modern world." it will pay more attention to its complete history. It is difficult to move forward without including 100% of an orchestra's history. I have been to Colorado since my journalistic sabbatical and look forward to a non-revisionist approval of all the chapters of its history!

Downplays/ignores conductors' tactics and brutality. They did not want to re-create the vision of Mozart and Beethoven. They wanted to dominate. Marvelous peyote button display but a very incomplete story. The labels are minimal—disappointing compared to Hard Rock Cafe.

Exhibition soft pedaled the vicious nature of Maestro Butrie's contact with the brass section. The American Conductors were brutal. His motivation was power; these were no campfire singalongs!

It was nice to see a description of the positive influence of classical music. Usually all you get is the tired line "classical music is for old folks". Overall, the classical music makes babies smarter. That isn't a PC view, but it is true.

10. Could you please tell us a little about yourself?

Katie Daltan, Age 9 ½

Global Trekker/Rabble Rouser/free spirit extraordinaire

My girlfrend forced me and my buddy to come.. becuz it's free??

I am a well-known music journalist specializing in High German Romanticism.

Thank you so much for bringing my music lessons to life. My great grandfather was an usher at Carnegie Hall and my great grandmother was one of Toscanini's many mistresses. I am BLESSED.

Our international delegation is honored to be here at the Klangmuseum of Vienna for the World Federation of Musicians Annual Meeting.

I hate old music.

Orchestra Bass Player, retired.

French Hornist, retired

Retired orchestra personnel manager and musician

11. Are there personal connections/reflections you would like to share?

The Principal Bass, Crowley, made it out with just a cut on his head. Relaxed as can be.

This is all so whacked. I thought a little peyote button would loosen up Mr. Tight Ass. He shouldn't have grabbed the steering wheel. What a scene!

The funny sign said sheep were playing music in the orchestra! Ha ha ha!!! :()

Okay this is the free exhibit, but very disturbing. The money/manpower/time/resources it took to bring an entire wrecked bus from America to Vienna leaves me very uncomfortable. In a starving world, I'm sure you could've utilized your resources a little more efficiently. How does all this old music relate to people today? Those musicians were assholes. So what? No wonder the conductor preferred sheep.

12. It is perfectly acceptable to find that there are some things you did not like about the exhibit. Would you be willing to tell me something you did not like about the exhibit?

it is quite stark: i miss them even more than i could have believed; and i was prepared to miss them a good deal. so this entry is really just a squeal of pain. it is incredible how essential to me they have become. i suppose you are accustomed to people saying these things. damn you, spoilt curator!

As the former personnel administrator, I am proud of what we accomplished. Were we perfect? Of course not. Do I regret the prostitutionalization of musicians' dreams? Sometimes, I do. The deforestation of millions of trees used for violins? You bet. But classical music makes babies smarter.

The animatronic orchestra musicians in the Virtual Podium didn't work with the cyber-baton thing they gave us. It was kind of broken/realistic.

A trap for tourists visiting to Vienna. The kiosk was just ok. The kids' concert was a joke. And the bus crash simulation was not good enough. Vienna has so much to offer, I would easliy skip this place and the rest of Veinna.

A lot of the texts were not very informative. There was little overall organization—or if there was any overall scheme, it wasn't explained. The wall texts assumed a lot of knowledge. Many artifacts, e.g. Musicians Apothecary, were hardly explained at all. I did like the exhibition; the fossilized musical instruments were fascinating. But the presentation was not, apparently, well thought through. Other exhibitions I've seen here were much better presented. Aboriginal art from India, for example, or in the Ocean Plastic Waste.

Great concept and beautiful objects but confusing layout. Would have been nice to have a bit more introduction at the beginning. It was also hard to find this exhibition since we came in the gift shop entrance. Need more signage at that end. Overall though, interesting show that was very sad.

I spent most of the time planning my escape route, i.e., avoiding creepy sheep puppet.

When we hit the rail Yup went clean through the windshield.

Ditch the background orchestra music.

13. Are there any additional comments you would like to make either about the Tutamen's Curse of the Maestro™ touring exhibit or about the museum as a whole?

The whole brass section was trying to tell Yup you can't get to Carnegie Hall from Interstate 70. Crowley Davids, that stoner bass player, was standing up in the front of the bus with him shouting Ride the snake, Dude! Yup was saying can you hear it? Follow the sound! Said it over and over. Could we hear it, could we hear it? Can you hear them clapping? All I could hear was like a farm animal getting spayed back in the conductor's lounge.

i hugged the map display. i like to waltz, you like to twerk. you and I are different people, but we are all linked in human history. this place makes the connection. take that connection home.

To be Viennese, is Hot. Very informational to see what the people of the United States have done with Our Music.

It was a long time ago. I honestly tried to go back and do due diligence. Hampered by the hallucinogenic Crowley said was cold medicine. I was able to free Parker and Crowley from the forward cabin before it burst into flames. This was not easy to do, bleeding, on my hands and knees, and only being able to see out of one eye. Members of the cello section had been assigned seats in the top deck. I could hear them screaming, unfortunately. Most of them were behind on their dues. Also, I did my best to save the Maestro. Was he a bad musician and a cruel and perverse human being? Certainly. But I did my best. Why? The same reason any highly trained musical artist gives up their artistry to play under a conductor in a symphony orchestra. Because that's what we're taught to do. Do your best. We are artists. I tried. What does that even mean? Bastard. Well, I was driven away by the flames. And barbeque smell.

First of all, most people don't even know that you can get in for free and second off all. No splash guards in the bathroom?? I rather pay full 25 dollars and get splash guards. Like really in a museum so big and so fancy you couldn't opt for splash guards?? "Get the splash guards maybe go up to a 2 star review."

I got shut out in a very rude way by a female security officer though there are 20 minutes left, which is bad because it's my last day in Vienna.

i still hear the Stonehaven Symphony playing in the distance—a sort of inharmonic, monotonous Aztec wail. i know they're in a better place now, a place where music critics are few and intermissions last forever. happy in heaven playing concerts where nobody ever messes up. if they did, the maestro wouldn't catch it. i feel the greatest peace and joy sitting in the empty auditorium not able to hear you your long cloak of silence like the goddess Indra studded with a thousand tin ears.

Getting the Chlamydia is free, too.

Thank you very much for your time.

AUTHOR BIOGRAPHY

G.T. Walker is the nom de guerre of Gregory Walker, a Black concert violinist and interdisciplinary artist (@electricvivaldi on Facebook and Instagram). He received a B.S. in Music with Honors in English at Indiana University followed by master's degrees in computer music and music composition at the University of California San Diego and Mills College, eventually collecting a doctorate and joining the faculty at the University of Colorado Denver's Department of Music and Entertainment Industry Studies.

Securing a publisher for his first novel, *Trigram Cluster Funk* (Double Dragon), winning the Elizabeth M. Cruthers Prize in Playwriting, and attending the Second Wind Theatre premiere of his science fiction drama *Chambers of the Heart*, he became a freelance writer and columnist for a number of national and international publications including *Strings, Hoosier Lit, Teen Strings, Points In Case,* and *Chamber Music Magazine*.

An American Academy of Arts and Letters Charles Ives Fellow, G.T. has been interviewed on National Public Radio and at the U.S. Library of Congress, and he was profiled in the internationally distributed documentary film, *Song of the Untouchable*.